Kate Fortune's Journal Entry

There's nothing like love in the air to keep an old body feeling spry! From the moment we met in Minnesota, I knew Adele O'Neil was just the woman that the Arizona Fortunes needed. You see, my first husband, Ben, left me some years ago when our marriage was in trouble, and had an affair with a Native American woman, which produced two sons. It took me some time to welcome these fine men into the family fold, but now I couldn't be prouder of them and their children. Adele has come to help the family realize our dream of building a children's hospital, but it's clearly more than business that's keeping my Jason by her side day and night!

Of course, Jason is a Fortune male through and through, and it's going to take him some time to realize that he's found the love to last a lifetime. But that boy better hurry, as I've got to help four other Fortunes find their perfect mates....

Dear Reader,

Silhouette is celebrating our 20th anniversary in 2000, and the latest powerful, passionate, provocative love stories from Silhouette Desire are as hot as that steamy summer weather!

For August's MAN OF THE MONTH, the fabulous BJ James begins her brand-new miniseries, MEN OF BELLE TERRE. In *The Return of Adams Cade*, a self-made millionaire returns home to find redemption in the arms of his first love.

Beloved author Cait London delivers another knockout in THE TALLCHIEFS miniseries with *Tallchief: The Homecoming*, also part of the highly sensual Desire promotion BODY & SOUL. And Desire is proud to present *Bride of Fortune* by Leanne Banks, the launch title of FORTUNE'S CHILDREN: THE GROOMS, another exciting spin-off of the bestselling Silhouette FORTUNE'S CHILDREN continuity miniseries.

BACHELOR BATTALION marches on with Maureen Child's *The Last Santini Virgin*, in which a military man's passion for a feisty virgin weakens his resolve not to marry. *In Name Only* is how a sexy rodeo cowboy agrees to temporarily wed a pregnant preacher's daughter in the second book of Peggy Moreland's miniseries TEXAS GROOMS. And Christy Lockhart reconciles a once-married couple who are stranded together in a wintry cabin during *One Snowbound Weekend....*

So indulge yourself by purchasing all six of these summer delights from Silhouette Desire...and read them in air-conditioned comfort.

Enjoy!

Joan Marlow Golan

Joan Marlow Golan
Senior Editor, Silhouette Desire

Please address questions and book requests to:
Silhouette Reader Service
U.S.: 3010 Walden Ave., P.O. Box 1325, Buffalo, NY 14269
Canadian: P.O. Box 609, Fort Erie, Ont. L2A 5X3

Bride of Fortune
LEANNE BANKS

Silhouette® *Desire*

Published by Silhouette Books

America's Publisher of Contemporary Romance

Special thanks and acknowledgment are given to Leanne Banks for her contribution to the Fortune's Children miniseries.

This book is dedicated to a couple whose love has stood the test of time. You keep teaching me. Happy 50th anniversary, Tom and Betty Minyard, aka Mama and Daddy.

 SILHOUETTE BOOKS

ISBN 0-373-76311-5

BRIDE OF FORTUNE

Books by Leanne Banks

Silhouette Desire

Silhouette Special Edition

‡ Sons and Lovers
* How To Catch a Princess
† The Rulebreakers
** Fortune's Children: The Brides
‡‡ Lone Star Families: The Logans
◊ Fortune's Children: The Grooms

LEANNE BANKS

is a national number-one-bestselling author of romance. She lives in her native Virginia with her husband and son and daughter. Recognized for both her sensual and her humorous writing with two Career Achievement Awards from *Romantic Times Magazine,* Leanne likes creating a story with a few grins, a generous kick of sensuality and characters that hang around after the book is finished. Leanne believes romance readers are the best readers in the world because they understand that love is the greatest miracle of all. You can write to her at P.O. Box 1442, Midlothian, VA 23113. A SASE for a reply would be greatly appreciated.

FORTUNE'S Children

Meet the Arizona Fortunes—a family with a legacy of wealth, influence and power. As they gather for a host of weddings, a shocking plot against the family is revealed...and passionate new romances are ignited.

JASON FORTUNE: The strong single dad had given up on love—until he came cheek-to-cheek with a *persistent* redheaded beauty who aroused an all-consuming desire....

ADELE O'NEIL: This beautiful hospital consultant came to Arizona to get away from the Minnesota cold, but she was going to have to melt the ice that had formed around Jason Fortune's heart to find the warmth she'd always sought!

LISA FORTUNE: Even a child could see that Adele considered her daddy a hunk—and Lisa knew Adele would make a great mommy.

KATE FORTUNE: This ageless family matriarch welcomed her husband's illegitimate sons into the Fortune family and her heart, but now she was hearing wedding bells for their children!

Prologue

The dream disturbed him so much that it woke him from a deep sleep.

He sat up in his large bed, his heart pounding, but Jason Fortune kept calm as he struggled to hang on to the vestiges of his visual. Fortune blood ran sure and true through his veins. He bore the weight and enjoyed the privilege. Although he hoped the strange visions were a product of indigestion, Jason would never deny that he was also a Lightfoot, Papago Indian, and wise enough not to ignore a dream.

Naked, he slid from beneath the Egyptian-cotton sheet and walked across the cool, polished hardwood floor to the wide window where the winter Arizona sky sparkled like diamonds.

Jason pondered the scattered images. Each evoked

a powerful emotion. There was no surprise he'd
dreamed about the Children's Hospital. The construction of Fortune Memorial Children's Hospital
was a matter of honor and pride and uppermost in
everyone's mind at Fortune Construction. His stomach twisted at the image that had followed—a bright
splash of blood on concrete. A threat. Protective instincts shot to the surface. He narrowed his gaze.
His younger brother, Tyler, didn't call him the lion
of the family just because he had amber eyes.

No time to comprehend the meaning of the blood
before the picture of Lightfoot's Plateau, long
thought to lend guidance in the ways of the heart,
had shimmered in his mind. Then a flame, warm and
exciting, sprang to life just before he had awakened.

A strange longing seeped through him. He had no
time for matters of the heart, he told himself. Being
vice president of marketing for Fortune Construction
and a single father to his precious daughter, Lisa,
filled all his hours.

If he sometimes felt a man's physical need, there
were women friends who accepted his lack of commitment. Every once in a while, in dark moments
like these, the teasing possibility that he could have
something more sneaked in. He always dismissed it.
After all, he hadn't found the bond he'd sought with
a woman even in marriage.

Matters of the heart? Jason rolled his eyes. He
rubbed his hand over his face and shook his head.
He headed back to bed, but the images of blood,
Lightfoot's Plateau and the flame taunted him. He
couldn't shake the sense that change was coming.

One

She would give anything for a bed.

Closing her eyes, Adele O'Neil leaned against the corner of Pueblo's crowded Saguaro Springs Country Club elevator and visualized the bed of her dreams—cool, crisp, cotton sheets, a soft, fluffy pillow and a snuggly comforter.

A man's baritone voice infiltrated her thoughts. His deep chuckle felt like velvet on her irritated nerve endings. She peeked through her eyelashes at the back of the tall, dark-haired man with the bedroom voice. Wearing a black suit, he transmitted a deadly combination of raw male confidence wrapped in a cloak of civilization. The flash of his white teeth contrasted with his tanned complexion. An unbidden image of the stranger reclining on her fantasy bed sneaked across her mind.

"You know what I think of committees," the man said. "If you want to get something done, do it yourself. If you don't, then form a committee. Especially one with an ethics consultant."

"Ethics consultant?" the man beside him echoed. "What's that?"

Adele strained to hear the answer.

"Somebody who presents all sides of an issue, which in some cases could take forever and make the committee lose sight of the original goal."

Poof. Adele frowned, and the image of the man in her dream bed disappeared. The man was partly right on the first count and totally wrong on the second. After her travel day from hell, the knowledge that she would be working with this man on the hospital committee didn't add any fuel to her engine. She wondered who he was.

He sighed. "But Kate has done a lot for us, and she is family, so I'll indulge her. I can handle Adele O'Neil."

Adele's blood heated. What an arrogant man. And what a shame that his arrogance was wrapped in such a nice package. She tamped down the urge to throw her shoe at him, but wouldn't want to hurt any innocent people standing next to him.

The elevator doors whooshed open, and the crowd rushed off. Blowing a wisp of hair from her eyes, Adele shifted the strap of the carry-on bag on her shoulder and trudged out. She noticed the way people stared at the two men who had been talking in the elevator, and it dawned on her who they were. Fortunes.

She could have smacked her forehead. She should have known. She'd seen enough Fortunes in action to recognize one when she saw one. Jason Fortune, she concluded, remembering the man who would serve on the ethics committee. Fortune power oozed from the gait of his walk to the formidable confidence in his speech.

I can handle Adele O'Neil.

His words echoed in her head, and Adele lifted her chin and located the powder room, ready to put on her battle armor. After five minutes of armor application, Adele was dismayed at the sight of herself in the mirror. "Miss Redi-kilowatt," she muttered. "One of these days, I'm going to shave it."

Her unruly red hair looked as though she'd stuck her finger in a light socket; she'd put a run in the fresh pair of stockings she'd packed in her carry-on; and her favorite lipstick broke. Adele snarled, then turned her back on her reflection and thanked her stars for a crush-proof little black dress and the good posture one of her caregivers had inspired by poking Adele between the shoulder blades every time she slumped.

Adele might not have everything the Fortunes had, but something told her Jason had never tangled with a scrappy Irish orphan like her before. Sometimes even big boys needed to learn some lessons.

Surveying the ballroom, Jason Fortune felt a measure of satisfaction at the occasion for the gathering—a motivational party given by Kate Fortune. Everyone involved with the plans for the hospital was present. For years his family had dreamed of building a children's hospital, and at last they were making the dream come true. He nodded at the faces of family, colleagues and employees and stifled an urge to yawn. As much as he respected and valued the familiar people present tonight, he struggled with a tinge of boredom. He appreciated the respect and deference afforded him, but every once in a while he felt a vague yearning for something more.

An odd current of electricity snaked up his back, and he turned at the sensation. His gaze immediately landed on a woman with wild red hair, sparkling green eyes, the pale skin of a Madonna and the mouth of a siren. She walked as if she owned the place, but Jason knew his family owned a piece of almost everything in town including the country club. Still, she reminded him of an Irish queen.

Feeling his brother's approach to his side, he nodded in her direction. "Who is she?"

Tyler shrugged. "I don't know. Kate seems to know her," he said as the *grande dame* embraced the redhead. "Looks like a lot of firepower in that one. Not your usual type."

Jason agreed. He generally preferred a quiet, agreeable woman, but he was curious.

Kate glanced up at that moment and waved him over. "My presence is required," Jason said, and walked toward the two women.

Tyler joined him. "Mine, too."

Jason slid him a look of disbelief.

Tyler lifted his lips in the trademark smile that

had stolen a hundred women's hearts. "I like red-heads."

"And blondes," Jason said dryly. "And brunettes and…"

"I have a deep appreciation for women."

"Just not for matrimony," Jason said.

"I watched and learned from you."

Jason frowned, thinking of his own experience with marriage. "Pick a different role model on this," he muttered, then stepped beside Kate Fortune and kissed her cheek.

"How are you darling?" She smiled at Tyler. "I hear the construction on the hospital is going well."

"Right on schedule," Tyler said, and glanced at the red-haired woman. "And who is—"

"Jason and Tyler, I'd like you to meet Adele O'Neil. Adele did such a good job at the hospital where my daughter, Lindsay, works in Minnesota. I'm delighted I was able to persuade her to be the ethical consultant for the new children's hospital here. You'll be working with Jason."

"Well, damn," Tyler said under his breath.

Jason nudged him with his elbow.

Adele smiled at Kate. "Kate, I've never heard of you not getting your way." She turned to Jason and Tyler. "The Children's Hospital is a wonderful project. I'm delighted to be on board."

Jason captured her hand in his. "We're delighted you've joined us."

She raised her eyebrows, and he saw a flash of disbelief mixed with challenge in her green eyes. "Oh, really?" she said. "You *like* committees?

Have you worked with an ethical consultant before? Some people have the misguided notion that an ethical consultant will present all sides of an issue, which in some cases could take forever and make the committee lose sight of the original goal.'' She shrugged her slim shoulders, drawing his attention down her pale throat to her full breasts. He wanted to step closer, to catch her scent. Instead, he held her hand.

''But I'm sure an enlightened man such as you would never hold such an ignorant view.''

She'd overheard him in the elevator, he realized. If she were Zorro, he'd have a big Z slashed across his shirt. When she started to remove her hand, he continued to hold it and rubbed his thumb over the inside of her wrist. ''If I did, I'm sure you could give me a different perspective.''

She gave him a second once-over as if reconsidering him, then nodded slowly. ''We'll see, won't we?''

More challenge, Jason thought, feeling the sensation rise within him like a threatening volcano. He allowed her to withdraw her hand and watched, with a flicker of irritation, as his brother edged in front of him. ''Nice to meet you,'' Tyler said. ''I'll be busy with the construction end of the hospital, so I won't be on the committee. But if you need anything at all while you're here,'' he told her, ''I'm your man.''

Adele's lips twitched. ''Thank you. I'll remember that.''

"Oh, Adele, here comes Sterling," Kate said. "You remember meeting him, don't you?"

"Your husband," Adele said.

Color rose in Kate's cheeks. "Yes."

Jason watched as the two women walked toward Sterling.

"Need me to pull the knife out of your gut?" Tyler asked.

"She's got a sharp tongue," Jason said, his gaze fastened on Adele. He struggled with the force of his strangely primitive and provocative feeling about her.

"Also got a great body," Tyler mused.

Jason frowned. "Aren't there about a dozen other women you've got on your fishing line?"

Tyler glanced at him in surprise. "You want this one," he concluded. "I haven't seen that look in your eye in a long time."

"What look in my eye?"

"Like you give a damn for a change," Tyler said. "You're always letting the ladies come to you. You look like you're ready to go after this one." Tyler studied him. "You look like you're on the hunt."

Jason opened his mouth to deny it, then paused. He'd made a policy to not get overly involved with a woman since his wife died years ago. Although sometimes his relationships with women met mutual physical needs, he always made it clear his commitment was to his daughter. His relationships with women had been carefully controlled and comfortable. Something told him any relationship he had with Adele would not be controlled or comfortable. In fact, the woman looked like a lot of trouble.

Jason conceded nothing. This was no one's business but his own.

Tyler shook his head. "It should be fun to watch. Have you declawed any cats lately?"

Adele felt Jason Fortune's gaze on her throughout the following hour. Although she tried, she couldn't dismiss the intensity in his amber eyes. She couldn't dismiss the man, period. Even though she tried to minimize his power and appeal, he clearly wasn't a man to be minimized.

He made her feel edgy, and there was no good reason for it. Sure, he was watching her, but she'd been watched before. Knowing that she would be in constant close contact with him to set up the parameters for the Children's Hospital made her stomach tighten with nerves.

Adele pushed back the sensation and drank the last swallow of champagne from her crystal flute. She felt light-headed and realized the combined effects of her tough travel day and just one glass of champagne were a clear signal it was time to get to the company condo she would be using. "I can handle this," she murmured to herself, "tomorrow."

"More champagne?" a deep voice inquired from behind her.

A quick jolt raced through Adele. Jason Fortune. "Oh, no. I just want a bed."

She glanced up at him and watched him pause. A whisper of a grin flashed across his face.

"I could probably help with that," he said, his tone rife with possibilities.

"I, uh, didn't mean it—" Feeling her cheeks heat, she took a quick breath. "I mean, I'm just tired. Long travel day. Thank you anyway, though." For Pete's sake! Adele wanted to kick herself. She had calmly faced more influential men than Jason Fortune without her mind flying away like a flock of geese. It occurred to her that he easily blotted out the rest of the room just by his proximity.

"I can give you a ride," he offered.

"Oh, no," she said. "That's not necessary. I'm sure there are other people you need to meet and greet."

He shrugged. "Not really. I tend to get bored at these events after the first fifteen minutes unless someone interesting walks into the room."

Surely he didn't find *her* interesting, did he? Surely she didn't want him to, she reminded herself.

"Do you have a car?" he asked before she could refuse again.

"Not yet," she admitted. "But I planned to get a cab."

"Not necessary," he said with an enigmatic grin. "I'll drive you."

Adele dropped all pretense. "I'm surprised you would want to spend one extra moment with the ethics consultant Kate has dropped into your lap."

"I'm not complaining," he said. "And you're not exactly in my lap," he added.

"But you weren't thrilled about it," she said, pointedly ignoring his spin on the lap comment.

"What would you say if I told you there is an old Native American saying that 'A man stands in darkness until someone brings him a candle'?"

"I would say *moo-moo,* this sounds like bull."

He narrowed his eyes, and for a moment she wondered if she had offended him. Then he gave a rough chuckle. "You're not what I expected."

"One thing I've learned from my training is you have to be careful about expectations. People and situations can be far different than your expectations. It's best to wait until the research is in before you make a judgment."

"And you've made no judgments about me," he said.

Adele opened her mouth, but her conscience chided her.

He dipped his head. "I look forward to this research. I believe you're staying in our condo at Saguaro Place. I'll call the valet for my car," he said, reaching for his cell phone. "Do you have luggage?"

Feeling uncomfortably outmaneuvered, Adele frowned. "Just a carry-on. The rest of my luggage didn't arrive with my flight. You know, you really don't need—"

He lifted his hand to halt her protest and pulled out his cell phone to order his car with a quiet voice. Then he cupped her elbow and guided her toward the door. Adele felt an odd tingling shoot up her arm. Within moments he'd retrieved her carry-on from the coat check, assisted her into his Jaguar and was pulling away from the country club.

"Tell me how you became an ethics consultant," he said.

She sank down into the leather upholstery and breathed in his scent. She noticed his large hands were capable on the controls of the car and his driving was swift but safe. Confident, she thought again, and very masculine. The package was surprisingly appealing to her, and when she was alone she would have to figure out what about Jason Fortune got under her skin—so he wouldn't get under her skin anymore.

"My specialty is setting up ethics parameters for children's hospitals and wings. I have a strong desire to protect children, and being a child in the hospital can be a frightening experience."

"Were you sick as a child?" he asked.

"No. I've always been disgustingly healthy. Strong Irish peasant stock, I suppose," she said with a little laugh.

"Then someone in your family?"

Adele felt the familiar dull emptiness echo inside her before she quickly, automatically set it aside as she had so many times before. How could a man surrounded by family understand what it was like to have none? "You've heard of Orphan Annie?" she asked. "Well, I was orphan Addie. My mother gave me up for adoption when I was very young, and I was raised in a children's home."

He glanced over at her, illuminated by a streetlight. "That must have been tough."

Although the feeling that she wasn't a "keeper" had haunted her much of her life, she refused to allow him to feel sorry for her, just as she refused to feel sorry for herself. "Growing up anywhere can be tough. I could have been raised in far worse conditions and been left in the dark about opportunities available to me."

He nodded. "Yeah. Some days my daughter, Lisa, makes growing up look easy. Other days, I can see it's hard for her."

Adele gave a doubletake. "You have a daughter?"

He must have heard the surprise in her voice. His lips twitched. "No prejudging from the ethics expert...."

"Okay," she conceded. "This may sound silly, but you don't look like a father," she said, then muttered, "whatever that means." Her stomach dipped at the realization that he might be married. "Your wife—"

"Is dead," Jason said.

"Oh, I'm sorry."

"It's been several years," he said quietly, and seemed eager to leave the subject behind. "So, what do I look like? Jack the Ripper?"

"No," she said. "You look like a super businessman-forever-bachelor."

"In that case, you would be confusing me with my brother. He has never been married and loves women in the plural sense."

"And you?"

"I am more selective," he said.

But no more committed, she guessed. "Why did you agree to serve on the ethics committee?"

"This is a family project. I have a passion for it. We all do. We're all very proud to make it happen. It's a matter of honor and of giving back to our people. As much as I sometimes get impatient with committees, I have enough experience to keep them from getting bogged down and not getting the job done. I am the best choice."

Her respect for him climbed a notch. "It must be nice to have always known where you stood with your family, to know that your position was understood and respected."

"My family hasn't always had it easy. We haven't always been so respected. You probably know that my father and his brother are the sons of Kate's first husband, Ben."

Adele felt a trickle of surprise. "Actually I didn't know that. I didn't ever understand the family connection, but there are so many branches to the Fortune family, I just accepted it."

"Ben and Kate hit a rough patch in their marriage when their child Brandon was abducted. Ben couldn't live with the guilt, so he moved to Pueblo for a while and focused on the Fortune Construction Company. While he was here, he met my grandmother, Natasha Lightfoot, and she helped him overcome some of his guilt and eventually reconcile with Kate. She also gave birth to Ben's twins. It took a while for Kate to accept my father and his brother, but after Natasha died, she did, and you know Kate, when she does it, she does it the whole way."

Adele nodded in agreement and smiled. "You're right about that. I can't believe how much energy she has." She studied his proud profile. "I wonder what your grandmother was like."

"She died before I was born, but I think she always felt caught between two worlds."

"But that's different for you?"

He glanced at her, his eyes stirring her with their intensity. "I'm Fortune and Lightfoot. My father has taught me to take the best from both worlds."

"You're very lucky," she said.

"There are also expectations," he told her. "And sometimes a man wants to be understood just as a man."

Adele's chest tightened. She could understand the need to be known as a human being. She supposed being a Fortune male could put a man in the position of being larger than life. Jason certainly seemed larger than life to her. It would take a brave woman to risk getting close to such a complex man, to know such a man intimately. *Brave* or *foolish,* she debated, and knew she wasn't the woman for the job. She didn't consider herself a coward, but she tried very hard not to be foolish, especially about men. Especially about a man who possessed qualities that would make him wrong for her. Adele preferred a more amiable, lighthearted, easy-to-manage kind of man, and she would bet her favorite shoes that Jason was none of those things.

Jason pulled to a stop. "This is your condo," he said.

Adele blinked. Usually, she was eager to drink in new sights and sounds. She'd been so caught up in her thoughts that she hadn't noticed anything outside the car. She'd been aware only of Jason Fortune. "Thank you," she said, determined to get away from the man who had so successfully distracted her. She quickly opened her door and reached for her carry-on.

"I'll take that," Jason said from behind her, and she felt the brush of the front of his thighs against her.

Adele felt another jolt at his nearness. "I can handle it. You've done too much already. I—" She broke off as he lifted the bag from her hands. He *would* be chivalrous, too, she thought darkly, and followed him up the walk.

"Your key?"

She almost gave it to him. His tone was somewhere between a request and a command. Instead, Adele reached in her purse and removed the key that had been sent to her. She was all too aware of his closeness, all too aware of how he watched her every move.

"You're accustomed to doing things for yourself, aren't you?" he asked.

"Yes," she confessed. "I've been told I can be independent to a fault."

"And what about men? What does it take for you to allow a man to do something for you?"

She wondered how he made the question sound both gentle and challenging. She slowly lifted her gaze to his and felt a restless sensation inside her. "I'm not sure. I have more practice with being independent." She tried to think, but she got caught in his amber eyes. "I don't know. Maybe trust, confidence..."

"Desire," he added.

Adele's breath stopped somewhere between her lungs and throat. The moment swelled between them, bringing an odd intimacy and sense of anticipation.

Jason lowered his head and brushed his lips over hers. Stunned, Adele stood stock-still. He slid his warm mouth from side to side, exploring her lips, trying her, then he slipped his tongue just inside her mouth. With a sensual invasion that promised heat and more, he kissed her.

Adele stiffened her knees, fighting the softening sensation. He pulled back and her mind reeled. What on earth had possessed him? Why hadn't she stopped him?

"Welcome to Pueblo, Adele," Jason said.

Two

Adele leaned against the inside of her door until her heart stopped pounding in her ears.

Welcome to Pueblo.

She'd heard of ladies who greeted newcomers with baskets of goodies, but she didn't think any of them looked or acted like Jason Fortune. And the goodies they delivered bore no resemblance to his kiss. She might as well have been whomped upside the head.

Mortified at her reaction to him, she covered her head with her hand. She'd even liked the way he tasted. This was ridiculous, she thought, whacking the door with her fist and moving away from it. Stupid. She simply could not get jelly-brained over Jason. She tried one of her power talk techniques.

"Ten reasons I shouldn't get romantically involved with Jason Fortune. One, I have an important job to do here and don't need the distraction. Two, he is not my type. He may be handsome and sexy and intelligent—" She broke off and swore. "He is not my type. Three, he is too confident. Four, he would not be easy to manage. Five, his eyes see entirely too much. Six, the way he kisses blows the roof off my head, and I like to be in control," she reminded herself. "Seven, he is a father and—" She faltered. *And I'm not good stepmother material.* This was another little dark spot in her soul. Since she'd had no parents throughout her childhood, Adele was extremely doubtful of her ability to be a good parent. After all, she'd had no role models. Because Adele couldn't contribute to a child with any parenting skills, she had devoted her life to improving hospital policies that dealt with children.

"Number eight, he's too sexy," she continued. If given the opportunity, she suspected Jason Fortune had the seductive ability to get her out of her clothes and into a lot of trouble in very little time.

"Number nine, he's too—" she hesitated, starting to run out of negative comments "—tall," she said triumphantly as she grabbed her carry-on and dragged it down the hall of the lush, contemporary condo. "Entirely too tall.

"Number ten," she whispered because it was a secret wish she'd never shared with another soul, "he would never see me as a 'keeper.'" As long as she could remember, Adele had wished someone would regard her as a keeper. Maybe someday, but she didn't dwell on it.

"Number eleven," she said, searching for a bonus reason as she stepped inside the spacious, well appointed master bedroom of the condo. The day settled on her head and body like a heavy cloak, and she sighed. "Oh, come on, Addie, you can come up with one more measly reason. His hair? His body?" She shook her head. She'd had to fight the temptation to run her fingers through his hair, and the Italian suit he'd worn hadn't concealed his muscular frame. She groaned, racking her brain. "He's a maverick," she finally said. "Mavericks are often uncooperative."

Takes one to know one, her conscience chided in singsong, but Adele drowned it out by belting out a Sheryl Crow song. As far as Jason Fortune was concerned, he was cooked. Stick a fork in him, he's done. Take him off the table. Adele had more than ten reasons why.

The following morning Adele awakened to the sound of someone pounding on her front door, quickly joined by the ring of her telephone. Stumbling out of bed, she grabbed the phone and ran to the door. "Hello," she said breathlessly to both.

"Luggage for Adele O'Neil," the delivery man said.

"Yes, thank you! I could kiss you!" she said.

"I accept the offer," the deep male voice on the phone said.

Adele's heart jumped. "Mr. Fortune?"

"Yes, yours is the best offer I've received this morning."

Feeling blood rush to her cheeks, Adele dragged the rest of her luggage inside and waved another thank-you to the delivery man. "I wasn't talking to you. I was talking to the man who brought my luggage. I was starting to get worried about it."

"So you trade kisses for luggage?" he asked.

She fanned her face to cool it down. "It was just an expression.

"If it's kisses for luggage, what do you give for breakfast?"

Adele squeezed the bridge of her nose, trying to make her brain move faster than sludge. This was not the kind of man a woman wanted to face in the morning before she'd had her first gallon of coffee. "I hadn't even thought about breakfast yet," she said, hedging.

"No need. I'll pick you up for breakfast at the country club in fifteen minutes."

Adele glanced down at her oversize Daffy Duck T-shirt in horror "Oh, no."

"No?" he repeated as if he were unaccustomed to hearing the word.

"I'm not ready for breakfast," she said, brushing a corkscrew curl from her eyes.

"You have no food in your condo," he countered.

That was true. She'd foraged through the cupboards last night and found nothing but some coffee for the coffeemaker and packets of salt. Her stomach growled. "Oh, thanks," she muttered at her recalcitrant body.

"Pardon?" Jason said.

"Mr. Fortune—"

"Call me Jason," he corrected.

Your Majesty might be easier. "I overslept. I'm not dressed for breakfast."

"How long would it take you to get ready?"

"Under normal circumstances, I could probably do it in twenty-five minutes, but—"

"Fine. I'll be there in twenty. 'Bye."

Adele pulled the receiver from her ear and stared at it. "Twenty! I said twenty-five under *normal* circumstances. This isn't normal. I need to pull out my suit of armor for this occasion and that takes an extra thirty minutes, and—" she glanced at the clock, and distress crowded her throat "—oh, peanuts, he's going to be here in eighteen and a half minutes."

Jason had barely lifted his hand to her door when Adele opened it. Her cool, wary, green eyes met his, and her lips did not lift into an easy smile. Most of her curly, red hair was pulled into a topknot while a few strands looked as if they were trying to commit mutiny by escaping. She wore a black suit that skimmed her curves and she held a leather folder under her left arm. If he didn't know better, he'd say she had a force field around her that NASA couldn't permeate.

"You look good in black," he said.

"Thank you." She walked in front of him toward his car, treating Jason to the inviting view of curvy backside. "I studied the psychology of colors, and I choose my clothing colors for what they communicate."

"And what does a black suit say?"

"It communicates reliability and projects a conservative image and authority."

"Don't mess with me?" he said.

Her green eyes warmed just a bit and her lips twitched, but she didn't allow herself to smile. "Possibly."

Jason opened her car door, then rounded the car to get in the driver's side. He noticed she opened the leather folder as he pulled away from the curb.

"Since you invited me for breakfast, I'm guessing you'd like to hear some of the issues we'll be covering on the ethics committee."

He watched her cross her legs and felt the slow drag of heat roll through him. Black stockings and heels. A wicked image taunted him of Adele dressed in black stockings and heels and nothing else. "That wasn't why I invited you to breakfast, but I wouldn't mind hearing what you've got planned. This is more of a personal welcome."

She shot him a wary glance. "I think you've done plenty of welcoming."

He saw her shift in her seat and found even that movement seductive. He gazed at her curiously. "Because we kissed," he said.

She shifted again and lifted her chin. "I guess I really should address that. We shouldn't have done that."

"Kissed," Jason said.

"Yes," Adele said, her cheeks blooming with color.

"You're blushing." Fascinated, Jason had to tear his gaze from her to watch the road.

"It's not polite to rub it in," she told him.

"It's so rare. I can't remember the last time I saw a woman blush."

"The curse of Irish skin," she muttered. "The point is we shouldn't have kissed."

"Why?"

She paused. "Because we're going to be serving on an ethics committee together. We have to protect our objectivity."

"From what you've said, it's our job to consider the issues from all angles. If we knew each other better personally, we would better appreciate the views presented."

A long silence brimming with disbelief filled the Jag. "Mr. Fortune," she finally began.

"Jason," he corrected.

She dipped her head, but didn't say his name. "I'm going to be very frank. It would be stupid for us to become involved. I sense very strongly that I am not your type. And you are not mine."

He admired her intuition at the same time that it annoyed him. "And what do you assume is my type?" he asked, deliberately keeping his irritation from seeping into his voice. He glimpsed a glint of fire in her eyes instead of intimidation.

"I'm going to guess your type is cool, sophisticated, intelligent, biddable perhaps to the point of being submissive. I'm not cool. My hair won't allow me to be sophisticated. I may be intelligent, but I just never mastered the ability to be biddable and submissive,'' she said with a smile that could either make him howl with arousal or cut him to ribbons.

"And what is your type, Adele?"

She took a slow, deep breath and exhaled. "I'm not sure I have a type, but if I did, I would say I prefer a man who is intelligent, compassionate and confident with a sense of humor and isn't—" She broke off as if she were searching for the right words. "I prefer a man who doesn't have any hang-ups about power or control, particularly controlling me.''

"You would say you don't have any hang-ups about power or control?" he asked, unable to keep the amused disbelief from his voice.

"I don't—" She met his gaze as he parked the car. "Okay, it's possible I might have some control issues, but I don't have a power problem.''

"Neither do I.''

She chuckled. "Of course not, Your Majesty.''

He paused, shaking his head at her. "You've got to be the most challenging woman I've ever met.''

She shrugged and lifted her hands. "See? Not your type.''

He reached for her hand and put his thumb over her pulse at her wrist, then pressed his mouth to her palm. Her pulse raced and her lips parted. "If you're not my type, then how do you explain your response to me?''

"I—I can't.''

"Ah," he murmured. "An unanswered question.'' He smiled wryly. ''My weakness. If there is a question I want answered, I will do everything in my power to solve it.''

She bit her lip. ''Is this your way of telling me you're hard-headed?''

''Persistent,'' he told her, still stroking the inside of her wrist with his thumb. ''Driven.''

''Then I guess you should know I'm no push-over.''

''I won't need to push you,'' he said. ''You are a woman with a strong mind and heart. Before all is said and done, you will come to me.''

She seemed to hold her breath for a moment before exhaling. ''Has anyone ever told you that your confidence is just a smidge over the top?''

''On the contrary,'' he said. ''I've been told my confidence is justified.''

Throughout breakfast Adele struggled to keep her attention fully on the material she'd brought with her. She tried, without success, to find a place on Jason's face that didn't distract her. First, his cheeks, but they were too close to his intelligent and seductive amber eyes. Then she alternately tried staring at his nose and chin, but they were too close to his mouth, and looking at his mouth reminded her of how he'd kissed her last night and the sight of his lips pressed against her wrist. It was all too easy for her mind to take the images further. He would be an incredible lover.

But not for her. Adele glanced down at her plate and saw that sometime during the course of the past hour, she had eaten breakfast. She wondered how it had tasted. Sighing, she closed her folder. "So as you can see, between the issues of teen pregnancy and determining what tribal customs can be permitted while the children are staying at the hospital, we have a lot of ground to cover."

"You're very thorough," he said.

"That's my job. The more thorough I am, the more smoothly and effectively the hospital will run. Thank you for breakfast."

"You'll want to get settled in today. If you need anything, give me a call," he said, and handed her a card. "You're invited for dinner at my house tomorrow night."

"Oh—" Adele automatically started to refuse.

"You're not afraid of me, are you?"

Adele blinked. "Afraid?" she echoed.

"Of your reaction to me," he clarified.

"Um, no," she said, but wasn't sure that was the truth.

"Good." He gave a slow smile that grabbed at her stomach and pulled. "I can drop you by the company car lot so you can get mobile."

As they left the country club restaurant, Adele noticed the surreptitious gazes he drew. She wondered if he noticed or took them as a matter of course. In a way he might as well be royalty in this town. He was a complex man, and if she weren't careful, she could very easily find herself fascinated by him. His confidence and intelligence were almost overwhelming, but she could have found a way to dismiss him if he hadn't displayed a sense of humor.

Especially about himself. The combination was almost irresistible, but she would resist.

Jason stood in front of the window, watching his six-year-old daughter, Lisa, play in the backyard. Her long dark hair flew behind her as she pumped on the swing. His mother was right. She'd been without a mother too long, but Jason still carried too much guilt from the death of Lisa's mother to get married again.

"Solving a world crisis or putting together another deal?" his mother asked from the doorway.

Jason turned at the sound of her voice and smiled. "Neither. Just watching Lisa."

Jasmine Fortune stepped beside him, putting down the shopping bag she carried. "She's the most beautiful six-year-old in the world."

Chuckling, Jason rubbed the back of his neck. "Some days she's six. Some days she's gunning for sixteen. I'll be fine until she turns thirteen."

"You'll be fine, period. You're a devoted father. It would be nice if you took another wife and gave your deprived mother more grandchildren, but—"

Jason shook his head. "You're getting me confused with Tyler again. I'm not the one who needs the marriage lecture."

His mother smiled sweetly and gave his cheek a peck. "Don't worry. I have enough marriage lectures to go around. I've learned from the best."

"Kate," Jason said.

"Of course. She believes it's her duty to make sure all the Fortunes are married."

"Whether they want to be or not," he muttered.

"Happily married," Jasmine said.

"Save it for Tyler, Mom."

Jasmine sighed. She lifted the bag. "I was at the store and saw a few things Lisa might like."

"Clothing or toys?"

"Just a couple of each," she said.

"You spoil her."

"And you don't?" she asked archly.

Jason tried not to spoil his daughter, but it was difficult. He always felt as if he were making up for the loss of her mother.

"What were you thinking when I came in? You didn't even hear me ring the doorbell."

"Cara," he reluctantly admitted. "I can't imagine my life without Lisa, but if I hadn't pressured her to have Lisa, she wouldn't be dead now. Her diabetes wouldn't have gotten out of control, and she would probably still be alive."

"And you would be divorced," Jasmine said bluntly. "She didn't love you the way you needed to be loved, the way you deserved to be loved."

Jason couldn't argue that the marriage had been unfulfilling for both of them, but he still would have protected Cara with his life.

"You've blamed yourself too long for this," Jasmine said. "You know Cara didn't take care of her diabetes during the pregnancy."

Jason jammed his hands in his pockets and looked out the window. There was no use discussing it. He couldn't bring Cara back, and he still felt responsible. He searched for another subject. "What's with this ethical consultant Kate has brought in?"

"I'll take the hint. You don't want to talk about Cara. Kate has only good things to say about Adele O'Neil. For some reason I expected someone more demure, but she's a firecracker."

"I agree with that," he muttered, remembering her sharp tongue and sweet scent. "What else do you know about her?"

"Not much. I understand she's not easily intimidated," she said, setting her shopping bag on the couch. "Tyler told me she took you to task over a disparaging remark you made in an elevator."

He rolled his eyes. "I apologized." He turned to study his mother. "This wouldn't be one of Kate's famous setups, would it?"

Her eyes widened in innocence. Jason couldn't tell if the expression was feigned or not. "I can't imagine that it would be."

"Good," he told her. "Because she's not a suitable wife for me or mother for Lisa. She has a temper and can be brutally blunt."

"Gorgeous hair, though," Jasmine said absently, then waved her hand. "But you're probably right. You might not be her type, either. Not every woman wants to marry a Fortune. By experience, I can tell you the men can be quite arrogant."

"And the Fortune women?" Jason asked, irritated with the similarities between his mother's words and Adele's.

"Are perfect," she said, pointing at Lisa. "See for yourself."

"You've always been too smart for your own good," he told her.

"I've had to be smart to keep up with your father." She glanced at him sideways. "This Adele, she really has gotten under your skin, hasn't she?"

Three

—

A good night's sleep and a set of reliable wheels worked wonders for Adele. The sporty sedan she drove toward the Fortune headquarters responded to her touch like a dream. She wore another black suit today that helped make her feel on top of things, and she was early. All these things helped her feel in control, and Adele had the uneasy impression that Jason Fortune had the ability to cause massive shortages of her control.

Adele refused to focus on that. The sun was shining, and she was going to have a terrific, controlled day. She glanced around her, taking in the different surroundings. Large saguaro cacti, aspen trees and paloverde grew beside the road. In the distance she saw low, rugged mountains. She braked at a stop-

light and noticed a car on the side of the road up
ahead. An elderly man was pulling something from
his trunk that looked like a jack.

Adele frowned. Although appearances could be
deceiving, Adele thought the man looked a bit unsteady on his feet. The light turned to green, and she
pulled forward slowly. As she drove past the large
sedan, she saw the flat tire and caught sight of an
elderly woman in the front seat.

"Darn," she muttered under her breath. This was
one of the rare times she wished she carried a cell
phone. Most other times she thought they were annoying and intrusive, which was why she refused to
carry one.

She pulled in front of the man's car and got out.
"Sorry you got a flat," she called to the man. "Can
I give you a lift somewhere?"

He shook his white-haired head, his gnarled hands
trying to turn a tire wrench. "No. Thanks, anyway,
but I've got to get my wife to Tucson for an appointment with her heart doctor."

If Adele remembered her geography correctly,
then she guessed Tucson was about twenty-five
miles away. She couldn't drive the couple and make
her appointment with Jason. She also couldn't, however, imagine leaving this man to struggle with
changing the tire.

"Well, uh, would you let me help you with that?"
she asked.

He smiled at her. "That's very nice of you, young
lady, but I can handle it."

A gentleman with a touch of male ego, she

thought. Her heart softened. She understood independence. She also saw that the man was having a tough time. "I'm sure you could handle it. I bet you've changed a lot more tires than I have. Your wife looks a little uneasy sitting here on the side of the road. She'd probably like you to hold her hand. Maybe you could give me instructions while you comfort her."

The man glanced at his wife, then back at Adele. "Are you sure you can do this? You're a little thing."

"But scrappy," she assured him, and extended her hand. "My name is Adele O'Neil."

The man's face lit. "Ah, an Irish lass. I'm John O'Malley. I'm much obliged."

"No problem," said Adele, kneeling next to the tire. "Let's hope your lug nuts aren't stubborn. Any tips?"

John proceeded to give Adele thorough instructions. Although Adele had taken a class on car repair and emergencies, she nodded throughout his suggestions. She was just fastening the lug nuts to the spare when, out of the corner of her eye, she caught the blur of another car pulling in front of hers.

She glanced at her watch and winced. Her chance to be early for her meeting with Jason had turned into "maybe on time by the skin of her teeth." "Almost—"

"Jason Fortune. Can I help?"

Adele heard Jason's smooth voice and broke a fingernail with the wrench. She rubbed her hair from her face. "Under control," she said, and wished she felt that way. She didn't look at him. "Almost done."

"Thank you, young man, but between the two of us, Adele and I took care of things. She just needed a little instruction from me."

"Instruction?" Jason echoed as if he couldn't imagine Adele accepting instruction from anyone.

"Did you say your name was Fortune?" Mr. O'Malley asked. "Is your family building the new children's hospital?"

"Yes, we are," Jason said. "Adele, let me finish—"

"I'm almost done," she said firmly.

Adele forced herself to pay attention to the task at hand and lowered the jack. She caught sight of his shoes and glanced away. She didn't like how aware she felt of him, as if she'd just eaten a dozen Twinkies and her pulse was racing from a sugar high. She tightened the lug nuts once more, then grabbed the tools and started to rise.

Jason steadied her with his hand under her elbow. She inhaled quickly and caught a whisper scent of musky aftershave. Feeling his gaze, she bit her lip at her body's response. She deliberately smiled at the elderly man. "I hope you make your appointment on time, Mr. O'Malley."

He took the tools from her and hobbled to the back of the car. "I'm sure we will, thanks to you."

Adele bade the man farewell.

"Why didn't you let me help you?" Jason asked as the O'Malleys drove away.

"Because I didn't need your help," she said, reluctantly looking at him. The combination of his strength, intensity and carved features did something to her. She had half hoped he would grow warts overnight so he would be less attractive to her.

"Why didn't you call the company auto service? They take care of this kind of thing all the time."

"Number one, Mr. O'Malley isn't employed by Fortune Construction. Number two, I don't carry a cell phone."

He stared at her in surprise. "You don't carry a cell phone. You've got to be kidding."

Adele brushed off her hands and walked toward her car. "No kidding," she said. "I think they're annoying and intrusive except during emergencies, and emergencies rarely occur."

He shook his head. "The company provides phones for key employees. We can get you wired in no time."

Adele frowned. "That's not necessary. I told you—"

"It's entirely necessary. While you are here in Pueblo, you are a key employee of Fortune Construction. If you should have difficulties with your car or need to contact me, then you will need a cell phone."

Adele sighed. "Are you this pushy with all your employees?"

"My employees are not this independent. This represents a safety issue."

He had a point. She hated to admit it, but he had a point. While she might dispute the key employee comment, Adele had to agree that if she had difficulties with the company car in unfamiliar territory, then she probably needed access to assistance. She made a face. "Okay, you're right. You win."

"Do you hate accepting help that much?"

Adele looked square into his lion eyes. "Don't you? If you had been changing that tire and I offered to help, would you have accepted?"

Jason paused a half beat. "No."

"Why?"

"Because I would want to finish what I started."

Adele nodded.

"And I would want to protect you from hurting yourself."

Adele stopped mid-nod, feeling an odd thud in her stomach as Jason's eyes searched hers. She was barely aware of the traffic that whizzed past them.

"You're not accustomed to having someone protect you, are you?"

She shook her head. "No. I'm not. I do my own protecting."

"Even the men in your life?"

There hadn't been that many men, Adele thought, and certainly no one on whom she'd felt she could depend. She shrugged and reached for her car door. "I do my own protecting."

Jason covered her hand with his, sending a dozen sensations through her. Adele glanced up at him.

"Maybe," he said in a voice that seemed to resonate inside her, "you need a different kind of man."

Ten minutes later Adele's brain recovered from the meltdown effects of Jason Fortune as she followed his Jaguar past the security gatehouse to the glass-and-marble building that housed Fortune Construction.

I don't need a man. That was what she should have told him when he'd opened her car door and assisted her inside. But her brain had scrambled from his touch, the sound of his voice so close to her and the seductive suggestion that she might need a man—a man like him.

She'd learned she didn't *need* a man to survive in this world. The question was whether or not she wanted one. Whether or not she wanted a man with enough confidence for ten men, a man who burned with passion, a man clearly at ease with his sexuality, a man who she sensed could make her burn for him. A man who would protect her.

Adele's stomach gave an odd flip at the thought. The strange feeling of longing surprised her. Was this some long-buried wish? It completely went against her code of self-reliance. From a very young age, she had learned she was in charge of protecting herself.

The idea, however, of having someone who cared about her health and well-being enough to look out for her struck at a soft, vulnerable spot inside her that she hadn't even known existed.

Adele frowned, wondering why Jason was affecting her so much. He seemed to have a knack for shaking up her natural order. He was just a man, she reminded herself. Sure, he was intelligent, charismatic and impressive, but he was just a man. Why did he seem more than that to her?

The tap on her window startled her. Adele glanced around and found Jason beside her car. Her heart tripped, and she took a deep breath to collect herself. Grabbing her leather briefcase, she unlocked the door, but he pulled it open.

"I'll walk you to your office," he said.

"I would think that Fortune's vice president of marketing might have more important things to do," she said gently.

He cocked his head to one side, looking at her in a considering way. "I believe you could be very important to the Fortunes."

Adele's stomach dipped. She couldn't tell if he was speaking personally or professionally.

He lifted his thumb to her cheek, and she froze. "What are you doing?" she asked.

His face was so close she could have counted his black eyelashes. He was close enough to kiss.

"You have a smudge from your angel-of-mercy duty," he said, then touched a strand of her hair escaping the upsweep she'd attempted this morning. "I like your hair better down."

"I wear my hair to suit me."

He tugged lightly at the strand, the barest seductive grin crossing his face. "I wonder what I could do to get you to wear your hair for me," he said. "Good question. Maybe we'll answer it another time."

He gently pressed his hand against her back and guided her toward the building. "After you get settled in, I'll introduce you to the attorney who will also serve on the ethics committee."

As they walked into the lush lobby adorned with Native American art and photos of beautiful buildings, Adele noticed heads turn toward Jason and people call out his name.

"What do you know about this attorney?" she asked as they headed for the elevators.

"Attorneys are a necessary evil. A project the scope of the Children's Hospital must be protected. The hospital won't be able to serve the community if it's not protected. That's what this attorney's duty is." They entered the elevator and he punched a button. "Something tells me hospital attorneys are not your favorite."

"You're right," she admitted. "But I agree with you that the institutions must be protected if they're going to serve and serve well. I've learned when I work with attorneys if I shift the focus away from what can not be done to *how* to do what needs to be done, we accomplish more."

"All in the questions," he said with a glint of mystery in his eyes.

"Yes," she agreed, but wondered what he was thinking. The man made her insatiably curious. He was both a puzzle and playground to her, and she struggled with the desire to explore him in every possible way.

He led her to her office and introduced her to a half dozen people along the way. Adele could see that he was respected and well liked. From her experience in the corporate hospital setting, she knew that combination wasn't easily achieved.

After a few more minutes, he glanced at his

watch. "I have a conference call in a few minutes, then some brief meetings. The attorney will arrive at eleven o'clock. My office is on the top floor."

"I'll be there at eleven. Thank you for showing me to my office."

He nodded. "My pleasure. What time shall I pick you up tonight for dinner?"

Adele's tongue wrapped itself into a knot. "I, uh—" she cleared her throat "—I decided it would be best not to join you tonight."

He watched her in silence, reminding her yet again of a lion, predatory, powerful, yet protective. He walked closer to her. "Do I make you uncomfortable?"

She opened her mouth to say no, but her mouth refused to form the word. "A little," she finally conceded in a low voice.

He nodded. "You make me a little uncomfortable, too," he told her, cocking his head to one side. "You disrupt me."

Relief swept through her. "Which means we should keep our relationship professional."

He shook his head. "That would be cowardly."

"Wise," she corrected, fighting a drop of panic. "Prudent, sane, sane," she repeated because Jason made her feel the exact opposite.

He shook his head again. "Cowardly. I'm curious about a woman with fire in her hair and eyes who changes tires for elderly strangers and fights for children. I think you're curious about me."

Adele bit her tongue, refusing to agree or disagree. She was tempted to plead the Fifth, but even that would have revealed too much.

"The invitation to dinner is open. You have my number. You can call anytime before six-thirty. I'll see you in a while for the meeting with the attorney," he said, and walked out of her office.

Adele sank onto the edge of her desk. "Oh, wow," she whispered. She was definitely out of her league. She hated the idea of being cowardly, and Jason was probably smart enough to know that. Yet he wasn't forcing the issue, just leaving the door to temptation wide open.

Adele wrung her hands and began to pace. Jason might be curious about her, but his curiosity would pass. She was certain she wasn't the kind of woman to hold his attention. She was either too much or not enough, but she knew she would never be a keeper for him. He would satisfy his curiosity, burn through her like a forest fire, then leave her scorched and charred.

She didn't like her choices in this situation. She would either have to be cowardly or prove to Jason that she was boring.

The lure hadn't worked. Jason glanced at his watch—6 p.m. He squelched the urge to insist that Adele join him for dinner. With the exception of his daughter, he couldn't recall an occasion where he'd found it necessary to insist with a female. He was accustomed to getting what he wanted when he wanted it.

"You're distracted," his father said to him. "Are you concerned about the Viceroy bid?"

Jason looked up to meet his father's gaze. "Not at all," he said, referring to the potential contract for a building for the largest law firm in eastern Arizona. "We're the best choice to give them what they want. I'll have that closed within two weeks."

Jason's father's hair was streaked with silver, his face chiseled with the same proud bone structure of his Papago mother, Natasha. Jason knew his father, Devlin, had weathered the slur of illegitimacy for several years before the Fortunes had embraced him and his brother Hunter. Together the two men had built Fortune Construction Company into a worldwide enterprise. Devlin inspired Jason's full respect if not always his agreement.

Devlin walked behind Jason and patted his shoulder. "You are an excellent hunter," Devlin said. "You're so smart about it most do not even know they are being hunted."

"I want them happy to be caught, so they'll continue to give Fortune Construction good recommendations." He glanced up at his father and saw mild amusement on his face.

"Your way with women is the exact opposite of your brother's," Devlin mused.

"I don't have a way with women," Jason said dryly, glancing at his watch. Adele wasn't budging.

"You haven't done much hunting with women. They come to you. Some women are easily seduced, but a prize requires patience."

"Mother talked to you," Jason concluded.

"Your mother always talks to me."

"About Adele O'Neil," Jason clarified.

"It's good for you to lose your indifference for a woman," Devlin said. "It's good that a woman can still make you feel."

Jason thought about Adele and felt impatient. He'd learned long ago there was only one way to take care of unanswered questions, and that was to do what it took to answer them. He would satisfy his curiosity about Adele. She might be under her skin, but he would allow her no deeper. "I won't be disrupted long," he promised, but he noticed when his watch turned 6:31.

Two days later Adele rubbed her finger over the cream-colored note card embossed with Jason Fortune's initials. It was the second note card she'd received from him.

Adele,
Are you enjoying your evenings in Pueblo? You are invited to dinner. My daughter will protect you if you are afraid. Call by 6:30 p.m.—Jason

She scowled. Although she'd successfully eluded Jason's invitations, she'd been bored out of her gourd. The comment about his daughter was low. It was 6:20, and she hadn't called him, but Adele found herself vacillating. What was she afraid of? She was curious about him, she admitted to herself. Perhaps seeing him in his home environment would eliminate his mystique, and then she could get past her heart palpitations and short breath every time he looked at her.

She glared at the card, willing it to give her an answer. Silly, she thought, and set it aside. She stuffed some professional journals in her briefcase and snapped it closed.

The clock taunted her—6:28.

Four

Adele rang the doorbell to the expansive South-western-style ranch home of Jason Fortune. Since it was Friday, she'd been told he and Lisa often escaped from their in-town home at Saguaro Springs to the ranch outside of Pueblo. Adele noted the distance between neighbors and thought the wide-open space suited Jason. He struck her as a man who immersed himself in his work and the community, but who also craved privacy.

She rang the doorbell again. When there was no answer, she found the door unlocked and stepped inside. Quickly taking in the comfortable surroundings of his home, she reminded herself she was here to get over her fascination with Jason. Hopefully there were many things not to like about him. She just had to find them.

"Too confident," she muttered to herself as she walked toward the back of the house. "Too handsome for his good and mine. Too controlled, too self-contained—"

She broke off her litany at the sight before her in the backyard. Jason, dressed in jeans and a T-shirt, stood beside a basket of softballs he pitched to a raven-haired little girl holding a bat and concentrating for all she was worth.

The intensity between them grabbed at Adele's heart. Heavens, what Adele would have given as a child just to know her father, let alone practice batting with him.

"Pitch, Daddy!" the little girl called.

Adele smiled at the impatience in her voice and watched as she hit a foul ball. "Good try," Jason told her, but she obviously wasn't satisfied.

Jason's daughter scowled and kicked at home plate. "Again," she yelled.

"Eye on the ball," Jason coached, and pitched a slow ball.

Jason's daughter whacked a grounder that whizzed through the clumps of desert grass and cacti in the backyard. The girl's face lit up and she hopped up and down. Jason gave a thumbs-up. "Great job."

Reluctant to interrupt, Adele watched several moments longer, drinking in the obvious affection between the two of them. Laughter, a little teasing, a lot of encouragement and a solid bond emanated from everything they said and did.

Jason had helped shape a daughter who possessed

his confidence and who had every reason to believe she was loved and lovable. Her heart squeezed tight. She wondered if either of them had any idea how precious that was.

Adele saw Jason glance at his watch, then at the house. He narrowed his eyes as he gazed at the doorway where she stood. Oops, she'd been caught. Watching him walk toward her, she opened the door and stepped outside.

"How long have you been standing there?"

"Long enough," Adele said with a smile, "to see someone working on Mark McGuire's record. She's terrific."

"I know," Jason said, then added wryly, "so does she."

"That's not all bad," Adele said.

"I know. It's just disconcerting when she seems to have the wisdom of a forty-year-old."

"Well, you know what they say," Adele told him. "Out of the mouths of babes, and as your daughter becomes a teenager I'm sure there'll be plenty of guys who will call her a babe."

Jason groaned. "Thanks for the words of comfort. Lisa," he called. "Come meet our dinner guest."

Lisa ran to the back porch and gazed at Adele curiously. "Are you the lady who is helping with the rules for the hospital?"

Adele smiled at how Jason had explained her job. "Yes, I am. My name is Adele O'Neil. You're a good hitter."

"I'm gonna get better," Lisa said.

"From the way you're practicing, I can tell you are."

Jason pushed open the door. "Let's get dinner. The housekeeper left a casserole in the oven."

"I hope it's nothing gross," Lisa said.

"Picky eater," Jason murmured to Adele as Lisa skipped in front of them.

Lisa lucked out. Tonight's fare was spaghetti pie. After dinner, the youngster was allowed to watch one television show before bedtime. While Lisa sat on the floor of the den, Jason joined Adele on the couch.

"You're still wearing your clothes from work," he said.

Adele nodded. "I didn't decide to come until late."

His lips quirked slightly upward. "It was 6:29. Has the evening been as much torture as you expected?"

She tossed him a sideways glance. "Not yet. This wasn't about torture," she said, although his closeness bothered her. "It was about being wise."

His amber gaze was intent. "What made you change your mind?"

Insanity. "I partially agree with you. Eliminate the curiosity and you eliminate the fascination." She prayed this was true. "Right?"

He nodded, his gaze falling to her lips, and Adele felt her mouth burn in response.

"Unless answering questions leads to more curiosity," he told her.

Heaven help her if it did.

Adele cleared her throat and glanced away from him. "I like your home. I bet you love being able to get away."

"My father says my two homes, just as his two homes, are a throwback to our ancestors' two-village way of life."

"And what do you say?"

"It's possible. All I know is I like the space." He paused. "I don't bring a lot of women around my daughter."

Adele's heart skipped a beat. "Why me, then?"

He gave a low chuckle. "Well, it's obvious you're not clamoring for a permanent personal position in my life."

Realization struck her, and she couldn't resist teasing him. "Oh, it must be a terrible burden dealing with all those Mrs. Jason Fortune wannabes. How do you do it?"

His gaze dropped to her lips. "Did anyone ever tell you that you have a very smart mouth?"

The phone rang and Jason answered it, providing her with an opportunity to breathe normally. Lisa's television show ended, and Jason motioned for her to get ready for bed. When the call extended past tooth-brushing time, he covered the receiver and said, "Crisis with one of our large accounts in the Midwest. I'll be a few more minutes."

Lisa, dressed in a white cotton nightgown that made her look like an angel, looked at Adele. "You want to read a book with me?"

Surprised and touched by the request, Adele nodded and allowed Lisa to lead her down the hall. "Sure."

"I'm too big to have Daddy do all the reading, so we take turns," she said as she climbed into her white four-poster bed. "You read a page, then I read a page. This is a book about a little girl named Junie B. Jones. She's very funny and she gets into a lot of trouble."

Adele joined Lisa on the bed and took in the way the decor combined femininity and pride in her Native American culture. Stuffed bears with pink ribbons and lace sat on a shelf next to a woven basket. Just as Lisa had suggested, they shared the reading of the entertaining book and were quickly finished. Lisa immediately turned her attention to Adele and hit her with a barrage of questions.

"Where did you live before you came to Pueblo?" Lisa asked.

"Minnesota," Adele said, tucking the covers around the child.

"What's it like there?"

"Much colder, wetter and very green. It's January so it's probably snowing."

Lisa touched a strand of Adele's hair. "Is it real?"

Adele raised her eyebrows. "What do you mean real?"

"One time Daddy went out with a lady and her hair was blond, but it wasn't real."

"Oh," Adele said, amused, thinking that must've inspired an interesting conversation. "Mine is real."

"How long is it?"

"A little longer than my shoulders."

Lisa sat up. "Can I see it?"

Disconcerted, Adele paused. Like father, like daughter? She relented, releasing her hair.

Lisa's eyes widened. "It's curly. Are they real, too?"

"Very," Adele said wryly. "I have done everything including ironing my hair to get rid of the curl, and now I've given up."

Lisa cocked her head to one side. "You're a lot different from the other ladies my daddy dates."

Adele pictured a string of cool, sophisticated, willowy blondes. "That doesn't surprise me," she said dryly.

Lisa leaned forward, her eyes wide with curiosity. "Do you think my daddy is a hottie?"

A hottie? Jason watched the exchange between Adele and his daughter from the doorway. He noticed Adele's hair hung in curly disarray to her shoulders. It looked as if his daughter was making better progress than he had. If he were a compassionate man, he would save Adele from the situation, but he wasn't feeling overly compassionate at the moment. He was curious.

"What do you mean by *hottie?*" Adele asked, dismay oozing into her voice.

"Ricky Martin is a hottie."

A long moment of silence passed. "Are you sure you're not a teenager?"

Lisa giggled. "Do you think my dad is a hottie?"

Adele stood and sighed. "I'm sure that many women think your dad is a hottie."

A hedge, Jason thought with a grin. He wondered if his too-smart-for-her-britches daughter would catch it.

"But what do you think?"

"I think he's an intelligent, fascinating man who loves his daughter very much." She paused. "I'm new at this. Are you stalling?" she asked, and the smile in her voice brushed over him like an intimate stroke.

"Yes, she is," Jason said. "And she's very good at it. Thank Miss O'Neil for reading the book and say good-night."

"Thank you for introducing me to Junie B. Jones and goodnight," Adele interjected in a cheeky voice before Lisa could.

Lisa giggled. "She doesn't always follow instructions, does she?" she asked her father.

"No, she doesn't," he said, tossing Adele a glance of mock disapproval.

"Thanks for reading with me. G'night, Addie."

"Addie?" Jason opened his mouth to protest the familiarity, but Adele shook her head. "Sweet dreams, sweetie."

Adele left the room, and Jason bent down to kiss his daughter's soft cheek. She wrapped her arms around his neck in a tight hug, and he felt a corresponding squeeze around his heart. Not a day went by that he didn't thank his lucky stars for Lisa.

"I like her," Lisa said, pulling back. "She's better than the blonde."

Jason kissed her again, cut the light and walked down the hall. He found Adele touching a decorative woven blanket that hung from the wall. It struck him that she was a tactile person. He wondered if she was also a tactile lover. He couldn't help wondering what kind of lover she would be. He intended to find out.

"It's from my grandmother's native tribe," he said of the blanket as he moved closer to her.

"It's beautiful. It must be wonderful to have all these things you can see and touch that show your family history."

Jason hadn't ever thought about it. "It's all I've ever known," he said, and realized that as an orphan, Adele had missed out on that. "Do you have anything that belonged to your parents?"

Adele shook her head. "The bracelet I wore in the hospital when I was born. So, all I got were their genes," she said, and shrugged with a smile. "Speaking of genes, your daughter is incredible."

Jason noticed the change of subject, but let it slide. "She can be a challenge. I didn't intend for you to have to read to her."

"I didn't mind at all. In Minnesota I would sometimes read to kids staying in the hospital."

He reached out to touch her hair. "I see she talked you into letting your hair down."

"Yes, it seems that both of you are a little fascinated by my hair."

"Tell me how she did it, so I can repeat it," Jason said, continuing to stroke her hair.

"How she did what?" Adele asked, giving him a glance that combined wariness and curiosity.

"How she got you to let your hair down," he said, feeling the heat that curled in his belly every time he was around this woman.

Adele closed her eyes for a moment, then met his gaze. "She's cuter than you are."

He chuckled and gave her hair a gentle tug. "Is that your way of saying I'm not a hottie?"

Adele's eyes widened. "You overheard!" she accused.

"You never answered her," Jason said.

"You are so confident that I'm sure the streets of Pueblo are lined with women who have told you in one way or another that they think you are a hottie. You don't need to hear it from me."

Adele was right about one thing. He didn't need to hear it from her. He'd rather her show him how she felt. Stifling a sigh, he shook his head. "Lisa was right. You don't follow instructions well. Come outside and look at our Arizona sky," he urged her, guiding her out into the backyard.

"It's beautiful," she said, looking up. "Away from the city lights, the stars look so bright."

"There's an observatory in Tucson. Maybe we can go sometime."

Jason saw her rub her hands over her arms and stood closer to her. "You're not accustomed to our change in temperatures."

"It's so warm during the day."

"But it really cools down at night. Have you satisfied your curiosity?"

"Some," she said, peering at him from beneath her eyelashes. "You've surprised me."

"How?"

"You really are a good father."

"What did you expect?"

"I expected you would have a nanny."

"I do," he admitted. "I'm a single father with a demanding job, so I don't try to do everything all the time. But you've met Lisa. I won't miss out on her growing-up years." He held her with his gaze. "But enough about me. You've had your turn. Now it's my turn to satisfy some of my curiosity about you."

Jason felt her tense slightly. "Okay," she said, but that one word was brimming with reluctance.

"Why aren't you married?"

"I'm not sure getting married is a good idea for me. I don't plan to have children so—"

"No children!" he echoed in amazement. "But you love children. You've chosen a career where you protect children."

"Yes," she conceded, "but that doesn't necessarily mean I'm great parent material."

Her comment turned his head around. "Why not?"

Adele gave a heavy sigh. "Because I don't know how to parent."

"None of us do," Jason told her.

"But you had role models," she said. "I didn't. In those moments when you have to make a split-second decision, you have training and instinct to fall back on. I don't have either of those."

He had no idea why, but it bothered the hell out of him that Adele truly didn't believe she had the potential to be a good parent. He crossed his arms over his chest and shook his head. "I'm not used to this attitude."

"You're used to women whose priority is to get married and have children. That's wonderful for them. It's just not for me."

"You have your career questions answered, but what about the personal ones?"

She looked unsettled by his question, then shrugged. "That's the great thing about life. You don't have to get all the questions answered at once."

He felt impatience burn and shimmer throughout him. He lifted his hand to slide his fingers through her hair and cup her jaw. "Then why do I want all my questions about you answered at once?"

She went very still, her gaze wrapped in his. "I don't know," she said in a voice so low it was almost a whisper. "I promise I'm very boring."

"I think you're lying," he said, and lowered his mouth to hers. Her lips were cool from the night air, but he felt the promise of warmth inside. He had the sense that this was a woman he could trust. This was a woman whose will and passion might just match his, but her passion was just out of his reach. He could taste her slight reticence and wanted to burn it away.

"This isn't wise," she whispered against his mouth.

"It's part of the curiosity," he told her, sucking on her bottom lip.

"But you've already kissed me," she said, her voice breathless. "You've answered that question."

"I'm still curious," he said, and slid his tongue into her warm, silken recesses. He explored her mouth, challenging her to respond. He tasted hesitation, then something inside her seemed to break free, and she kissed him back.

She met him stroke for stroke, and her breasts brushed against his chest, teasing him. Sliding his hands down to the back of her waist, he urged her against him.

She tasted and felt like pure feminine passion, and he was hard with wanting. The desire went deeper than sex, but he couldn't comprehend another way to express it. She drew something incredibly elemental from deep within him. She opened her mouth to him, tugging sensually on his tongue, sending a flash fire of raw desire through him.

Skimming one hand upward, he cupped her breast and rocked his lower body in the notch of her femininity. Her little moan was like gasoline on the fire, and he felt the edge of his control fray.

Devouring her mouth, he pushed his hands down to her bottom and tugged her skirt upward. He slipped his fingers inside the silk of her panties and stroked her bare skin. "You feel so good. But I want more," he muttered, and touched her intimately. Touching her there with his hands only succeeded in making him want to be inside her, stretching, pumping.

Adele shuddered and turned her mouth from his, gasping for air. Pushing against him, she stumbled backward.

Jason instinctively reached out to steady her, but she held up her hand and shook her head. Her eyes dark with arousal and a sliver of fear, she continued to shake her head. "I told you this wasn't wise."

Still throbbing with his need for her, Jason stepped toward her to reassure her.

"No," Adele said. "I didn't come here tonight to be seduced." She bit her lower lip, swollen from his kisses. Even that small evidence of their passion aroused him further. "Although, I realize you may not have been able to tell that by the way I responded to you."

He noticed she wasn't denying her response, and that was one more confirmation that she would match him. "My daughter is inside sleeping. I didn't intend to seduce you tonight."

"Not tonight, but sometime?"

He raked his hand through his hair. "It's inevitable that we will make love, Adele. There's something unusual between us."

Her eyes grew wide. "It is not inevitable. We're two rational adults. We might have gone a little crazy a few moments ago, but we both have a choice in the matter. Just because we went a little crazy once, doesn't mean we have to do it again."

"Once?" he prompted, reminding her of the first night they met.

She shrugged. "Okay, well I figured that other time you kissed me was some sort of local custom."

Jason swallowed a chuckle. "You're not going to try to rationalize this, are you? I thought you were more honest than that."

She looked at him, her gaze shimmering with passion, agreement, fear and reluctance.

"I want to know you," he said, "in every way. I won't be satisfied until I know you in every way. You are the same way. I can feel it when I touch you. Can you honestly tell me you'll be satisfied in choosing to not know me?"

She took a careful breath. "I'll have to be."

Five

———

"Ten kinds of crazy," Adele repeated to herself over the next several days. She was ten kinds of crazy if she got sexually involved with Jason Fortune. The man seemed to bring things out in her she hadn't known existed. Longings inside her that alternately screamed and whispered. The desire wasn't the worst. She had felt desire before, although it had never overwhelmed her. No, it was the whispered reminders of secret dreams she'd abandoned years ago that bothered her most.

Jason belonged. In every way that Adele had ever wanted to belong, he belonged, yet stood on his own. She was drawn to him both for his strong sense of self and equally strong sense of family. He exhibited an incredibly powerful balance of individuality and connectedness. She secretly envied that balance, because she sure as heck knew she didn't possess it. He held an important place in his family's minds and hearts. He was also a protector in the same way she was, and Adele knew on a deep, gut level, that Jason was strong enough to protect her. She'd never met a man like him.

Embarrassed by her abandoned response to him, she'd been reluctant to face him again. Fortunately, he'd been out of town on business Monday. Today, however, she'd been summoned to meet him in his office. He was taking her to the hospital construction site.

His secretary waved her in his door. "Go on in. He's down the hall. He'll be back in just a couple of minutes."

Adele walked into his office and immediately felt the essence of the man who spent hours here. Although she'd been in his office before, Jason had dominated her attention. Alone, she stole the opportunity to drink in everything she could learn of him.

A desktop computer occupied one corner of his large walnut desk. Assorted files were stacked neatly on the other side with a spreadsheet on top. A leather date book and complicated telephone that looked as if it would do everything but make coffee testified to a busy schedule.

Two photos of Lisa greeted him throughout his day. Adele felt a tug inside her. His daughter would be there on those occasional rough days when he looked at those photos and found his reason for doing all that he did.

Adele glanced at the wall and walked toward a large colorful Native American print. A group of Indians looked as if they were gathered in celebration.

"Saguaro Wine Festival by Michael Chiago," Jason said from the doorway, drawing her attention from the print.

Adele felt her heart dip at the sight of him. He wore his dark suit with ease, and his crisp white shirt contrasted with his tanned skin. The expression in his assessing amber eyes made her heart dip again. He had held her and touched her. He wouldn't forget it. Nor would she.

She cleared her throat and forced her attention back to the print. "What is Tohono O'odham?"

"In the eighties, the Papago decided they wanted to be known as Tohono O'odham. It means desert people. My cousin, Shane, feels strongly about using the Tohono O'odham name, but Tyler and I still think of ourselves as Papago because that's the name we grew up with." He walked toward her. "Did you know saguaro wine was the first wine made in America before the Europeans arrived?"

She hazarded a glance at him and saw the slight grin on his face. "And they actually make it from the cactus?"

"From the fruit of the saguaro."

"I don't believe I've ever had saguaro. We don't seem to have a lot of them in Minnesota."

"It tastes like a combination of fig with a hint of strawberry."

"And the wine?"

He chuckled. "Let's just say it packs a punch."

Beside the large print was a smaller picture of a cave on a red-rock plateau. "And this?"

"Lightfoot's Plateau," he said with a thoughtful expression on his face. "The cave within the plateau is believed to be able to provide guidance in the ways of the heart. It's a spiritual place that used to belong to my grandmother's family. Others own it now."

She heard the disapproval in his voice. "And you're not too happy about that," she ventured.

"None of my family is pleased. We want it back." His gaze embodied rock-hard determination. "We will get it back."

Adele didn't doubt it. She wouldn't want to be the opposition in a battle with the Fortunes. They were a formidable group. Geez, just trying to keep her wits with Jason was enough for her.

He looked at her. "But that's for another time. Now we visit the hospital."

Adele joined Jason in his Jaguar as he drove to the construction site on the outskirts of town. Situated on several acres, Fortune Memorial Children's Hospital was on its way to becoming a sprawling, modern, fifteen-story complex.

Adele felt a stirring sense of satisfaction knowing that she would help make the operation of the hospital successful. "It's very impressive," she said. "And it's not even finished yet. How proud does it make you feel to look at it?"

He met her gaze, and the light in his eyes drew

her like a beam in the darkness. "This will be our greatest accomplishment."

He barely helped her out of the car before Tyler was calling his name. A wide grin split Tyler's handsome face as he gave each of them a construction hat. "I'm ahead of schedule," Tyler said triumphantly. "We're halfway done."

"Have you told Mom and Dad?" Jason asked.

"I thought I'd save the good news for when I see them tonight, just as they start to apply the matrimonial screws to me again." He turned to Adele. "Is my brother giving you enough trouble?"

Adele couldn't help smiling. "More than enough," she said and waved her hand. "The hospital looks great."

"You haven't seen nothing yet. Wait till—"

"Mr. Fortune," a worker called. "Problem here."

Tyler shrugged. "Duty calls. Jason will have to do the tour. Stay away from the west side of the building. Some men are working on the fourteenth floor, and I don't want you to catch any falling hammers. I'll try to talk to you before you leave. Later," he said, then walked back to the site.

"Later," Jason said to his brother, then took the construction hat from Adele's hand and put it on her head. "Stay close and watch where you walk," he instructed.

"It looks like both you and Tyler are very safety conscious about the site," she said, noticing the fences and warning signs posted throughout the site.

"Fortune Construction has an excellent safety

record. We've never been investigated by the Division of Occupational Safety and Health, and we plan to keep it that way." He frowned as if something disturbing occurred to him. "If it's humanly possible, there will be no injuries with this project."

The attitude was consistent with Jason's protectiveness. It extended to both his family and his employees. She wondered at his tone. "Has something happened to make you concerned about the possibility of accidents?"

He stopped and looked at her. "No. Why do you ask?"

Adele shrugged. "I don't know. Something in your voice."

Hands on his hips, he glanced away, looking as if he were debating something. He rubbed his chin. "A few weeks ago I had a crazy dream with a lot of powerful images. One showed blood at the construction site."

Adele felt a chill. "What did you do about it?"

"It was just a dream," he told her, "but where Tyler was doing double checks on safety, I told him to start doing triple checks."

She nodded and they began to walk forward again. "Have you and Tyler always gotten along well?"

"Mostly," Jason said. "We had the usual sibling rivalries. Athletics, academics, cars…" He glanced at her. "But never girls. I married young."

"But you've been single for some time," she said.

"I hate to admit it, but I'm probably the reason

Tyler won't get married. He saw the pain my marriage caused and he just thinks love hurts too much. When it comes to women, Tyler is into volume." He tossed her an assessing gaze. "What do you think of him?"

Surprised by the question, Adele blinked. "I don't know him well. He seems nice, and conscientious about the construction of the hospital."

"Would you say he's attractive?"

"Of course," Adele said, dodging some scraps of concrete. "But he's not like you."

Jason stopped, and she plowed into the back of him. "Oops. Excuse me"

His face was inches from hers, making her heart slam against her rib cage. "How is he not like me?"

She tried to get her brain out of neutral. "Uh, he, uh, he doesn't have your eyes."

"Eyes," he murmured. "What color are his eyes?"

"I don't know," she said, feeling as if she could drown in his amber gaze. "They're just different from yours."

He smiled. "They're gray," he said. "Tyler's eyes are gray."

Adele took a quick step backward and inhaled deeply. "Thanks. I'll remember that," she said, and hoped there would never be a quiz. She blew a strand of hair out of her face and resolved to change the subject. She tried to call up some of the research she'd done before arriving in Pueblo. Diabetes, she remembered. "About the hospital, will you have specialists in diabetes?"

The humor left his face. "Yes."

He turned around and walked ahead, leaving Adele to blink at his change in demeanor. She frowned, walking after him. "Excuse me," she said to his broad back. "Did I just step on a land mine or something? I think the temperature dropped from a hundred degrees to subzero. If I said something wrong, I'd like to know what it was."

He hesitated, but didn't look at her. "My wife died of complications of diabetes soon after Lisa was born. By the time Lisa was born, there was irreversible damage to Cara's kidneys." He clenched his fist. "I couldn't do anything."

His last four words were full of masculine anguish. Adele's heart softened. The protector had been unable to protect his wife. Jason was such a strong man with equally strong character. How unbearable that must have been for him. Adele couldn't not reach out to him. She tentatively touched his arm. "I am very sorry," she said.

He glanced at her, and the recognition of his pain seemed to vibrate between them. He wouldn't quite accept her comfort, she could see it in his eyes. Adele, however, understood that, too. She couldn't explain to herself or anyone else at the moment, but she hated that he bore this alone.

"You mentioned diabetes because you've done your homework," he said, closing his hand briefly over hers before he removed it from his arm. "What other specialists do you think we'll have?"

"Mental health and treatment of alcoholism?"

Jason nodded. "We plan a large mental health

and prevention department, both inpatient and out-patient. Also diet and health education. We'll co-ordinate with tribal medicine men and women and—''

"Ladies who pray," she said, pulling out a tidbit of information she'd gathered on the Internet.

Jason smiled in approval. "Very good. What else do you know about the local reservation?"

"It's the second largest in the United States."

He nodded. "Did you know they lease some of the land to a casino?"

"You got me there."

"Then you have a few things left to learn," he said, his gaze a mix of masculine mystery and sen-suality.

A lot left to learn, Adele mentally corrected as she tried to keep herself from emotionally sliding right into Jason's arms and drowning in him.

Jason didn't understand that for Adele he might very well be the most dangerous man in the world. He embodied all her abandoned wishes and dreams. Wishes and dreams she'd clung to, but abandoned for the sake of survival. He was a constant tempta-tion and could easily become a constant craving.

Adele knew in the bottom of her heart that sex with Jason would never be just sex. She knew she would give more and open herself to more in a way she'd never experienced. She knew that loving him would irrevocably change her, and Adele wasn't ready for that change.

In celebration of the ahead-of-schedule progress of the construction of the Fortune Memorial Children's Hospital, the management sponsored a quickly organized picnic late Wednesday afternoon for everyone connected with the project. Picnic tables loaded with food lined a scenic area of Four Corners Park, a beautiful public park with bicycle and jogging paths, a field appropriate for soccer and baseball and a playground boasting a variety of equipment for children.

Although Adele had successfully avoided Jason during the last hour, she found her gaze drawn to him time and time again. Many employees sought him out, and he appeared to give each person his undivided attention. That was one more thing to admire about him, Adele thought, and she already had too many.

"Adele, darling," said Kate Fortune. "How are you adjusting to Arizona?"

"The weather's wonderful," Adele said. "I can see why you and Sterling prefer to spend your winters here."

"I do miss the green after a while," the ageless wonder said. "Ah, there are Jason's parents. Devlin, Jasmine, did you meet Adele at the cocktail party?"

Adele watched the handsome couple walk toward them and took in the curious expressions on faces that echoed some of Jason's qualities. "Briefly," Devlin said, "but we've heard much about her."

Oh, goody, Adele thought wryly.

"From Jason, Tyler and Lisa," Jasmine added with a tinge of sympathy. "I'm not sure Kate warned you that you would have your hands full dealing with my son. He's a hard taskmaster and very thorough.''

"Adele is very thorough, too," Kate assured Jasmine. "If anyone's up to the job of handling Jason, she is. Right, Adele?"

Adele paused and decided to redirect. "The Children's Hospital is a terrific project. I'm excited about setting up the parameters of operation for the hospital." Out of the corner of her eye she caught sight of Lisa playing catch with an older child next to the bike trails. "Jason has done a wonderful job with her. Is she afraid of anything?"

"Unfortunately, no. She adds new gray hair weekly," Jasmine said, but there was pride in her face. "She thinks she can do anything."

"And she can," Devlin pointed out.

Jasmine smiled at him. "I believe she inherited some of her grandfather's confidence."

"Lucky girl," Adele said, the assessment popping out without forethought.

Devlin glanced at her thoughtfully in a way that vaguely reminded her of Jason's intensity. There was such respect and love among them. For a brief moment she wondered what it would be like to belong to such a family. The thought rubbed at a vulnerable part of her, a part she kept secret. It almost hurt to open herself to the possibility, so she quickly pushed it aside. "I'm sure you're proud of both your sons," she said.

"Ah, yes. Tyler," Kate said, and made a tsking sound. "What are you going to do about his single status?"

Jasmine and Devlin exchanged a look of determination. "Devlin and I have discussed this thoroughly, and we're in agreement on how to handle the matter. We have everything under control," Jasmine said firmly.

"Well, if you need any help," Kate offered.

Devlin's lips twitched and he patted Kate's hand. "We'll let you know."

Just then Tyler let out a loud whistle. "Attention, everyone! I want to thank everyone who is giving their best to this project and keeping us ahead of schedule. Give yourselves a round of applause."

As everyone applauded, Adele caught sight of a blur in her peripheral vision. She glanced quickly to the side and saw a racing bike whizzing around the corner. Just ahead, Lisa stepped into the bike path to catch a ball. Adele called out her name, but Lisa couldn't hear. Lisa's dark, silky pony tail swung behind her as she watched for the ball with her father's concentration in her gaze.

Adele's heart leaped into her throat. Instinctively her feet took flight, and she pushed Lisa out of the way of the bike. She felt her hands on Lisa's back and felt a rush of relief. The child was safe. She caught a flash of metal glinting in the sunlight just before the bike careened into her side. Pain shot through her, and she fell. Her head hit the ground, and everything went black.

Jason saw a crowd gathering near the bike trail. "What's up?" he asked Tyler.

Tyler shook his head. "Beats me. I was getting ready to get in line for a burger."

"She's been hit," a man called. "We might need an ambulance."

Jason's gut tightened. "*Who's* been hit?"

He ran to the scene and wove through the crowd. He spotted his mother with her arms tightly clasped around Lisa. Where was his father? "Who?" he demanded.

"I dunno," someone said, craning to see over the people. "Some redhead."

There was only one redhead in the park. Adele. His stomach fell to his feet. He pushed through the rest of the way and saw Adele lying on the ground. His father was waving aside an apologetic teenager next to a bike.

Jason rushed to Adele's side and bent down. She was pale, and her eyes were closed. "What happened?"

"She saved me!" Lisa said, her voice welling with tears. "He was gonna hit me, but she pushed me out of the way."

"Are you okay, baby?"

Lisa nodded, but buried her face against his mother's waist.

"She's unconscious but breathing," his father said. "I'm not sure anything is broken."

He focused exclusively on Adele, taking in the scrapes on her legs and arms. Fighting a dozen wild emotions, Jason touched her face, and she let out a soft moan. "Wake up," he urged, hating that she was hurt. "Please wake up."

She turned her head from one side to the other and winced.

"Adele," he said again.

Her eyelids fluttered. She looked at him and grimaced. "Ouch."

A sliver of relief trickled through him. At least she was conscious. "Where does it hurt?"

She lifted her arm to cover her eyes. "Oh, God, where does it not hurt?" she whispered. She licked her lips. "My toes don't hurt. My neck doesn't hurt. My face—" She paused. "My face is too close to my head for me to know if it hurts or not. Is Lisa okay?"

Jason exchanged a look with his father. She was obviously in pain, yet she was concerned about Lisa's safety. Moved, he took a careful breath. "We need to get you to the hospital."

She rolled her head from side to side and winced. "No hospital," she said, "just my bed."

Jason frowned. "Don't be ridiculous. We have to get you checked by doctor."

"No. I'll be okay," she insisted, and struggled to sit up. "See? I can sit. I don't need to go to the hospital." She continued to gingerly hold her head while drops of blood fell from her elbow to the pavement. "I just feel like I got hit by something." She blinked several times as she met his gaze. "A bike," she said. "A very fast bike."

"I'm taking you to the hospital," Jason said grimly.

"I don't like hospitals."

"Is she always like this?" his father asked in a low voice.

"Just every minute she's awake," Jason muttered, and braced her for fear she would faint. "Adele, you work for a hospital."

"That doesn't mean I have to like them." She narrowed her eyes and lifted one knee.

"What in hell are you doing?" he demanded, horrified.

"I'm getting up." She looked him directly in the eye.

"No, you're not," he told her firmly.

"Yes, I am. If you're not going to help, get out of my way." She made a sound of exertion as she tried to push upward.

"Adele—" He broke off and swore. He slid his hand behind her back to support her. As soon as she made it to her feet, the crowd began to applaud.

She gave a weak grimace that passed for a smile. "I want to go home," she told him in a low voice.

"Look after Lisa," Jason said to his father.

"An unusual woman," Devlin Fortune said for Jason's ears only. "She has the heart of a lion."

Jason only knew she had saved his daughter. He would protect her now.

Six

"You tricked me," Adele said.

"I brought you home," Jason responded, standing to get rid of some of his edginess. The memory of her lying on that concrete still shook him.

"But you also pulled in a favor and got a doctor to make a house call." She shook her head. "I told you I was fine."

"Fine doesn't exactly cover it. Dr. Feore said your hip and shin are severely bruised, you have a mild concussion and numerous scrapes. Why do you fight being treated by a doctor?"

Adele shrugged. "It's probably habit. At the children's home where I grew up, we had spills all the time. Doctor's visits were reserved for big things like broken bones, surgery and stitches. If we cried, someone would inevitably make fun. That tends to make you a little tougher.''

Her response bothered him. The whole situation bothered him. He wished she'd had a different growing-up experience, that someone had taken better care of her. She'd deserved that. Still unsettled that she'd been hurt, he sat next to her outstretched legs on the sofa. "I wish I'd seen the bike," he said. "You shouldn't have been hurt."

Adele rolled her eyes, then crooked her finger in invitation. "Come here."

Jason cautiously scooted closer. When she began to unbutton his shirt, he went completely still. The fleeting, teasing touch of her fingertips reminded him of how she'd felt when he'd kissed her. When she stopped, he felt like a yo-yo, swinging from one emotion to another.

Her hint of a grin was both sexy and gently wry. "I didn't think I would find an undershirt with a big *S* for Superhero. You can't be everywhere at once. I was just there at that particular moment. I saw what was happening. I didn't do anything anyone else wouldn't do."

That was where Adele was wrong. "I haven't met many women eager to run into the path of a racing bicycle to save my daughter."

"I guess you just haven't met many of us tough Irish broads, then."

Amused by her description of herself, he gave a short chuckle. Her skin was porcelain-white with just a hint of sun on her nose, and her frame small but sturdy. Her hands too were small. He ran his fingers over the soft skin of one of her hands, then laced his fingers with hers. He liked the fit. "I guess I haven't." He met her gaze and lifted her hand to his lips. "Thank you."

Her eyes darkened with the same emotion he felt echoing in his gut. She closed her eyes and shook her head. "Don't look at me that way, as if I'm something special to you when I'm not."

"What if you are?"

She opened her eyes. "It's temporary. It will last as long as a sand castle during high tide, probably not even a full night."

Irritated, he thought about arguing with her, but took another tack instead. "I didn't know you were that fickle."

She gave a double take. "Me? What do you mean me?"

"You said it would last as long as high tide."

"I was speaking of your interest in me."

"Why would you presume to know that?" he asked. "You don't know me well enough."

Clearly disconcerted, she opened her mouth, but her doorbell rang. Jason went to the door and opened it to his mother and Lisa.

His mother lifted her shoulders helplessly. "Lisa was so worried about Adele that she insisted we check on her."

Holding a foil-wrapped plate, Lisa squeezed past him and scurried to Adele. "I brought you a burger and chips and pickles, a gelatin dessert and a brownie." She made a face. "Nana added some gross potato salad because she says adults like stuff like that. Did you break anything?'' she asked, curiously looking over Adele's arms and legs as she presented the plate of food.

"Not a bone,'' Adele said with a smile. "How did you know I was starving for a burger, chips, pickles, gelatin, a brownie and potato salad? Did you read my mind?''

Jason saw a rare trace of shy pleasure cross his daughter's face.

"I just guessed,'' she said. "Thank you for saving me. I'm sorry you got hurt.''

Adele's eyes softened, and she reached out to touch Lisa. "You are very welcome and very worth it. Besides I just got a few scrapes.'' She pulled the foil off the plate. "You want some of these chips?'' Adele asked as she and Lisa headed to the couch.

"She's very good with Lisa,'' his mother mused.

He heard the familiar speculation in her voice and shot her a warning glance. "Don't read anything into it.''

"I may not be the one you need to worry about,'' she said with a nod in the direction of the sofa.

Jason caught sight of Lisa sitting in Adele's lap while they shared the meal. Ambiguous feelings pulled him in different directions. Seeing his daughter soak up the attention of a woman who could have been her mother reminded him of all that Lisa had missed. At the same time he wanted to save Lisa from the loss she might feel when Adele returned to Minneapolis. "I don't want her to get too attached.''

"You may be a little late for that,'' his mother said. "It's hard not to get attached to someone who saves you from a terrible accident. Especially when she has red hair and shares her brownie.''

His mother had a point. It was hard not to get attached to the woman who had saved his daughter. ''Lisa, you should go home with Nana now. Adele needs to rest.''

Adele raised her eyebrows. ''I do?''

Lisa giggled. ''She doesn't always follow Daddy's rules.''

''That's probably good for Daddy,'' his mother murmured, then smiled at Lisa. ''Come with me, sweetie. Adele, thank you for filling in for Lisa's guardian angel.''

Adele's cheeks bloomed with color. ''You're welcome. Now that's enough. No more thank-yous. I appreciate the food.''

''I hope you feel much better tomorrow,'' Jasmine said with a wave, and led Lisa out the door.

After they left, Jason turned to face Adele.

''You can go, too,'' she said. ''I'm fed, bandaged and safe. There's nothing else you can do for me.''

His lips twitched. ''Is this your sideways way of saying my presence isn't needed?''

''This is probably going to be difficult for you to understand, but I've been taking care of my scrapes and bruises most of my life, and I've done a pretty good job.''

''Did you ever wish you could take a break from it and let somebody else do it?''

Her eyes flickered with a hint of secret longing, then she glanced down, and her eyelashes shielded her expression from him.

"Did you ever wish there was someone you could trust to take care of you every now and then?"

She lifted her head and met his gaze a shade defiantly. "You mean did I ever wish I had someone I could depend on?" She nodded. "Of course I did. But I wasn't raised in your wealthy situation. When I say wealth, I don't mean money, I mean wealth of family. So, wishing for someone I could depend on could be a very dangerous wish. Don't seduce me with your family when what you really want is a one-night stand."

Anger, swift and hot, shot through him. "You disrespect both of us when you say all I want is a one-night stand. How can you think one night would be enough?"

Adele inhaled sharply. "Jason, when it comes to you, I don't know much. That's why I don't want to get involved. We both know we're not interested in anything permanent. So tell me what you're shooting for here. Something more than one night but less than forever?"

Her question was so right and wrong at the same time that it made him want to howl in frustration. Jason had spent years developing his self-control, and the idea that Adele could shatter it so easily upset him even more. When had a woman had an impact on him like this?

"I'm making you totally crazy, aren't I?" Adele asked.

"Yes," he said as he counted to one hundred.

"Good," she said. "At least we're even on that."

Raking his hand through his hair, he debated kissing her and decided against it. His control was too frazzled. As much as he wanted to disrupt her the way she disrupted him, this wasn't the time. "I want to kiss you, right now," he told her. "I want to make love to you until the only thing you can say is my name. But you're sore from the accident and not convinced about us. Both those circumstances will change. If you need me for anything," he said, "anything at all, call me."

The silence in her house after Jason left was the same kind of stunned quiet she would expect after a bomb explodes. His energy and passion reverberated inside her for moments after he left.

Adele spent the rest of the evening wandering around her condo, surfing channels on the television, then turning it off and wandering some more. She went to bed early in search of some of that rest everyone insisted she needed, but she only tossed and turned.

Glaring at her alarm clock at midnight, she cursed Jason Fortune for disturbing her life and sleep. Adele made a snap decision and impulsively dialed Jason's office number. She knew no one would pick up and she would get the voice mail, which was exactly what she wanted. In no mood for any more confrontation, she left a message telling Jason she was taking the day off and she would return to work on Friday.

When Adele hung up the phone, she turned off the ringer and felt a rush of relief. Tomorrow would be a Fortune-free day.

The decision worked like a charm. She fell asleep and even slept in the following morning. She felt stiff upon rising and bored after an hour of puttering around the condo. Adele missed Minneapolis and all the familiar things that made her feel secure. Although the condo was well appointed, she realized she'd been so busy she hadn't added any touches of comfort.

She headed for a local nursery she'd spotted during one of her many trips to the Fortune offices. "Can I help you find something?" the sales clerk asked.

"I'm just interested in picking up some house-plants," she said. "I'm from Minnesota, so I miss the green."

The clerk nodded sympathetically. "We have a wide variety. You may need to water some of them a little more frequently, but they'll still thrive."

"Thanks," Adele said, and turned down an aisle.

"Did I hear someone say Minnesota?" a somewhat familiar female voice asked. "Is that you, Adele?"

Adele turned to find Jasmine Fortune smiling at her. Adele struggled with a yeah/boo sensation. Jasmine was so friendly and vital it was a pleasure to see her, but she was also Jason's mother, and Adele was doing her best not to think about Jason today.

"Mrs. Fortune," Adele said.

"Call me Jasmine," she instructed. "Between your work for the hospital and rescuing Lisa, you're practically part of the family."

Adele felt a surge of pleasure out of nowhere and

reminded herself that *practically* was the operative term.

"You're here for houseplants."

"It may sound silly, but I miss my plants. I think more green in my condo might make me more at home here."

"A little homesick," Jasmine said, and put her arm around Adele's shoulders. She glanced down the aisle thoughtfully. "We can't have that. Do you want something that blooms?"

For the next hour Jasmine, in her friendly, embracing way, helped Adele select a miniature forest for her condo. "I hope I don't kill them all," Adele said at the checkout.

Jasmine reached for her purse. "Why don't you let me give them to you as a welcoming gift?"

"Absolutely not," Adele said, a little more sharply than she intended. She deliberately softened her voice. "I owe you because you made sure I got some potato salad last night."

Jasmine laughed and shook her head. "That's the most original turndown of an offer for a gift that I've ever received. Would you join me for lunch or do you need to get back to work?"

"I took the day off," Adele said, and although she wasn't sure it was wise in the long run, she didn't have the heart to refuse Jasmine a second time.

"Kate's been very enthusiastic about you," Jasmine said as the two of them sat at a table in a charming café near Four Corners.

"Kate is a marvel," Adele said, "and when she's

sold on something or someone, she's the most generous person I know."

Jasmine nodded. "I know she struggled with the fact that her husband had fathered Devlin and Hunter by another woman, but ever since she pushed aside her reservations, she's been gung-ho in her involvement with the family. The woman is a born matchmaker. She's determined to see every unattached member of the family happily married."

"Is Tyler on the top of her list?"

Jasmine arched an eyebrow. "Tyler is on the top of everyone's list. He's dodged the commitment bullet, but I'm pretty sure that will change soon."

Adele sipped herbal tea. "Has he met someone?"

Jasmine smiled. "If he hasn't, he will." She waved her hand. "Enough about that. Tell me about yourself."

"I'm originally from Minnesota. I graduated with a double major in philosophy and prelaw, then picked up a master's degree in business ethics."

"I already know you're eminently qualified. I'd like to know more about your interests and your family."

Adele squelched a trace of nervousness. It was silly, but she didn't want Jasmine to think less of her because of her lack of family. "My job has kept me very busy, but I like to swim and fish when I get the opportunity. In Minnesota I volunteered by reading to kids in the hospital. No family. I was raised at the local children's home where I coached volleyball until I left."

"No family," Jasmine repeated. "Then I bet all

these Fortunes must feel a little overwhelming at times.''

''At times,'' Adele admitted. ''But for the most part, I think the Fortunes are lucky to have each other.''

''We are a close family, but my sons are very private about their personal lives. I'm a mother, so I worry about both of them. Jason got married young and was forced to grow up quickly. Of course, Devlin and I married young, too, but that was very different,'' she said, and her beautiful features turned pensive. She looked down and tapped her finger on the table. ''Sometimes I think Jason buries himself in his responsibilities for Fortune Construction and Lisa.''

The humanness of Jasmine's concern for her grown son affected Adele deeply. There was no prying, meddling attitude, instead Adele could feel Jasmine's love and tenderness like a warm breeze. She had the oddest urge to comfort her. ''Your son is a strong man,'' she said simply. ''You obviously did a wonderful job raising him.''

Jasmine met her gaze and slowly smiled. ''Devlin and I would agree that we got great raw material to work with when we got Jason.'' She cocked her head to one side thoughtfully. ''You have a good heart, Adele.''

Adele's heart swelled in her chest. The quick joy took her by surprise. No one had ever complimented her on her heart before. Her mind, yes, her discipline and perseverance, yes. But never her heart. In fact, Adele had always received the vague impression that it was always best to follow her head instead of her heart. For that sliver of a moment it was as if she had a mother who had praised her.

It felt as if she'd just been given a rare gold coin. "Thank you," she said, but the words seemed inadequate.

The following day Jasmine's words stayed with her, and she couldn't help seeing Jason in a different way. The two of them spent the afternoon setting preliminary policy for the teen pregnancy center.

"I really admire your commitment to this issue. Some children's hospitals don't want to touch it."

He leaned back in his leather chair and tossed his pen on the desk. "We couldn't not touch the issue. My grandmother, Natasha Lightfoot, was nineteen when she became pregnant with my father and his brother," he said, then paused and looked away. "My wife became pregnant the first time when she was nineteen."

"The first time?"

"She miscarried," he said, and Adele sensed, as she always did, that Jason's wife was a difficult subject for him. He looked at her, and she could tell by the glint in his gaze that a subject change was coming. "My mother told me she had lunch with you yesterday. I asked her what was her secret."

"Secret for what?" she asked, clueless.

"Secret for getting you to join her for lunch," he said.

Adele felt a rush of warmth from the hint of edgy but controlled passion she saw in his eyes. She wished she didn't identify so easily with that same edgy passion. She wished she felt more control.

"So what is her secret?" he asked.

Adele's mind went blank. "I, uh—" She bit her tongue to stop her blasted stammering. "She doesn't affect me the same way you do," she blurted out, and immediately wanted to melt into the Southwestern carpet beneath her feet.

He gave a wry smile that was entirely too sexy. "I suppose that's good."

Adele glanced down to avoid Jason's gaze and caught sight of her watch. She gasped. "I didn't realize it was so late. It's 6:30. I bet your daughter's going to jump you when you get home."

Jason shook his head as if he saw through Adele's diversionary tactic. "Lisa's already attending a combination birthday, slumber party at a friend's house."

"Oh," Adele said, feeling her stomach do strange things at the expression on his face.

"I thought dinner at—"

The phone rang, interrupting him. Jason frowned. "Who would be calling at this time?" he muttered, then picked up the phone. "Jason Fortune," he said. His eyes widened in shock. "An accident at the hospital construction site?" he echoed.

Adele watched his face grow taut, and her blood turned cold through her veins. Jason stood and walked toward the window. "Was anyone else hurt?"

Adele's heart sank. She watched Jason hang up the phone, his entire demeanor shrouded in shocked grief. "There's been an accident at the site," he told her in a too-calm voice. "The temporary service elevator crashed. Our construction foreman, Mike Dodd, was in it. He's dead."

"Oh my God," Adele said. "What—"

"I need to go to the site right now," he said, raking his hand through his hair. "But I also need to call the other members of the board."

"Would you like me to call them?" she asked, desperate to help.

He gazed at her as he decided. He nodded. "Yes, I would. Here are the phone numbers," he said, pulling a short list from his top drawer. "Tell them we don't have many details yet and they'll be updated within an hour." Jason grabbed his suit coat from the back of his chair and shook his head. "Just like that he's dead."

"Did you know him, the foreman?" she asked.

Jason nodded. "Primarily as an employer. Mike had a rowdy youth, but he really seemed to have started to pull things together. Being foreman for the hospital project was very important to him." He sighed, and she could see the weight of responsibility settling on his shoulders. "The next few days are going to be a nightmare. A death at the hospital construction site." He closed his eyes for just a moment. "We've never had a death at a construction site before." He opened his eyes and met her gaze, turmoil and determination mingling in the depths of his amber eyes. "The board members are going to have three thousand questions, and believe me, I've got four thousand."

"I can stay here and be the phone tree when you want to give an update. If you like, I can call Lisa so she won't be alarmed."

"Good idea." He checked his watch. "It'll be late, and it's a Friday night."

"There is really nothing I'd rather do," Adele said.

"Okay," he said, and the power of trust hummed between them. He could count on her. The knowledge shifted something inside her. More than anything, she wanted him to count on her. She wanted to be the one on whom he could depend.

Her heart in her throat, she watched him head for the door. "If there is anything else I can do, anything at all, please tell me." He looked so strong, so grieved and so alone in that moment that she could hardly bear it. After all the hours she'd spent with Jason, she knew how important this project was to his family, and even more so, to him.

Following her heart instead of her head, she stepped toward him, put her hands on his arms and kissed him. He kissed her hard in return, then left, and as Adele watched him walk down the hall, she had the impending sense that everything in her world was about to change.

Seven

At the construction site, Jason parked his car behind
a collection of vehicles with flashing lights. A police
cruiser was parked behind a fire truck. An ambulance was just pulling out of the drive.

Jason's gut clenched. The ambulance was probably carrying Mike Dodd's body. The nightmare had
begun. He narrowed his eyes and caught sight of his
brother talking to a policeman.

Jason approached them both. "Jason Fortune," he
said, introducing himself to the policeman.

"Officer Crowther," he said. "You two broth-
ers?" he asked.

Tyler nodded while Jason continued to look
around the site. It was difficult to believe they had
all been celebrating the progress on the hospital just
two days before.

"I was just telling your brother that since there was a death there will be a full investigation from both the police and the Division of Occupational Safety and Health."

Jason knew the investigations could cause extensive delays in construction.

"There are always questions to be answered in these cases," the officer said.

"Believe me," Jason said. "We will want those questions answered more than anyone else. Could you excuse my brother and me for a moment?"

"Sure," he said, and Tyler and Jason walked to the construction trailer that housed the site office.

"What was Dodd doing at the site so late?" Jason asked as soon as he shut the door behind him.

Tyler looked gutted. Jason had never seen his brother so shell-shocked.

Tyler shook his head. "I don't know. Everyone else had left. Maybe he was checking something. It looks like the elevator fell from the fifteenth story."

"So no one else was here?"

"No one except Angelica Dodd, Mike's sister, and Riley."

Confusion rocked through him. Riley Fortune, their cousin, was vice president of finance for Fortune Construction. Jason wrinkled his brow. "Riley? His area is finance. What in hell was he doing here tonight? Have there been some financial discrepancies?"

Tyler shook his head again. "Not that I know of. The only thing I know about Angelica is that she pretty much raised Mike and she's a waitress at the

Camel Corral. Maybe she knew he was working late and was bringing him something to eat.''

"Did you have any idea there were problems with the elevator?" Jason asked.

"There have been no problems with the service elevator," Tyler said adamantly, and swore. "If there was one project I didn't want messed up in any way, it's this one. I don't know how this could have happened.''

Jason knew how important this project was to Tyler. He also knew his brother had been routinely working seven days a week to make sure everything went smoothly. "This is not your fault. We'll call the company lawyers, and I promise we will find out what happened.''

"It's Friday night," Tyler said doubtfully. "We might have a hard time getting the lawyers.''

Jason flipped through his small book of numbers. "They're on retainer. We pay them to be available.'' He punched out a number. "We sure as hell aren't going to wait for outside investigators to wade through their paperwork to get the answers we need. Too much is at stake here.''

He couldn't help remembering the odd dream he'd had, and the blood at the construction site. He shuddered at the knowledge that the image had become true.

A half hour later, after he'd talked with Officer Crowther again, he called Adele to give an update. Her voice felt like water when he'd been stranded in the desert. "There's too much we still don't know," he told her. "We already have an attorney on the site. Tyler's scouring daily construction reports, and I've spoken with the press. Could you tell my mom it might be best if Lisa stays with her for a few days? I'll be working round the clock.''

''Of course,'' Adele said. ''What are you doing for food?''

''I haven't even thought of it,'' he said.

''Then don't,'' she said. ''I will.''

''You don't need to do anything else. You can go home now,'' he told her and they hung up. He wondered why the simple act of talking to her and hearing her voice made him feel as if he'd just gotten a second wind. He shook his head. God knew he didn't have time to figure it out now.

A little later, a security guard entered the trailer with a bag of food. Appearing slightly harried, he looked at Tyler, Devlin, who had appeared moments ago, and him.

''Yes?'' Jason prodded expectantly.

''Which one of you is Jason Fortune?'' the guard asked.

''I am.''

The guard dug into the bag, produced a wrapped sandwich and handed it to him. ''A pretty, but pushy redhead made me promise to put this in your hand. She said there are a few rainbow sugar cookies in there too.''

The guard left the bag on the desk and exited the office while the three men sat in silence. The atmosphere in the office had been thick with unrelenting tension, and the guard's words cut through it like a knife.

Tyler snickered. "Pretty, pushy redhead. Wonder who that could be."

Jason shook his head, but couldn't help cracking a slight grin. "I told her to go home."

"She probably did," Tyler said, "after she went to the deli and harassed the security guard. Hand me that bag."

Jason tossed him the bag and felt his father's knowing gaze. His father's eyes saw more than the deli sandwich and a flustered security guard. He saw Adele's unrepentant determination to look out for Jason's welfare and her ability to add a breath of levity in an incredibly dark moment, and Jason saw it, too.

The grueling night continued. Jason appeared on television the following morning, then joined the board for an emergency meeting. Take-out meals mysteriously appeared, delivered, he was told, by a redhead. Late the following evening he finally went home and grabbed a few hours of sleep.

On Sunday he met with Link Templeton, an investigator with outstanding credentials. Jason immediately clicked with the man with the observant hazel eyes. Link exuded an air of confident experience, and Jason felt a measure of relief that Link would get to the bottom of the incident.

It was dark on Sunday evening as he drove toward his home. Still restless from the events of the last days, he rejected the idea of going home and turned instead toward Adele's condo.

She opened the door and he drank in the sight of her. A silky robe covered her from head to toe, her face was scrubbed clean of make-up, her hair hung in soft curls to her shoulders and her large green eyes searched his. "Come in," she said without hesitation.

Before he'd seen her he'd felt raw from the aftermath of the accident. Now, he felt raw from his desire for her. He closed the door and immediately took her into his arms.

He felt her gentle probing gaze on him in the soft light of her foyer. "How are you?" she asked.

"Well fed," he said dryly. "How many times did you bring food to the site?"

"A few," she admitted. "I figured you would forget to eat unless it was put in front of you."

"You were right," he said. "How did you get to the guards?"

"Persistence," she said. "And cookies."

He chuckled and slid his fingers through her fragrant hair. "Rainbow sugar cookies. My father liked them."

She smiled. "Good."

He felt as if he'd waited an aeon to kiss her, and he couldn't wait a second longer. He lowered his head and took her mouth. The taste of her raced through him like fire, and he was immediately aroused. At another time, he thought, he could have gone more slowly and seduced her. She deserved the time and the seduction. He forced his mouth away from hers. "I can't do this slowly now," he said in a voice that sounded rough to his own ears. "If you want me to leave, tell me now. I'll count to ten."

Adele just stared at him and the seconds ticked past, echoing with the pounding pulse in his brain. A sliver of fear flashed in her eyes, and she closed them tight, but still said nothing.

The time passed, and she finally opened her eyes. The fear had been replaced with hot desire that played over him like an intimate touch. Jason slid his hands beneath her robe and pushed it from her shoulders. She stood before him totally naked.

Adele wondered if she would ever breathe again.

Heedless of her nudity, she slipped her fingers through his silky black hair and drew his mouth to hers. Jason spun them both around until she felt the cool wall at her back and his heat everywhere else. He devoured her with his lips and claimed her body with his hands.

She struggled with a trickle of fear. His passion was so powerful she wondered if he would consume her until there was nothing left of her. She had never known a man could hunger for her like this. She had never known she could hunger for a man like this.

When she'd seen the strain on his face, she'd wanted to take it away. Adele pushed aside the fear and followed her heart. She tugged at the buttons to his shirt and urged the jacket and his shirt off his shoulders.

Jason pulled back and stripped the clothes off his upper body. Gazing at her with eyes full of fire, he swept her into his arms and carried her to the bedroom. He spilled her onto the bed, then the condoms from his pocket, and shucked his slacks and briefs.

His chest rippled with strength, his abdomen was

washboard flat, and between his powerful thighs, his arousal jutted out large and hard. He followed her down, covering her like a warm blanket.

"I have wanted you since the first time I saw you," he said, and sucked gently at her bottom lip while one of his hands traveled down to fondle her nipple. The sensation of his hard body and his hands and mouth made her grow damp and swollen.

"Why?" she asked breathlessly. "Why me?"

"You were stronger than any woman I'd ever met." He trailed his other hand down coaxing her legs apart and touching her intimately. "I had to have you," he said, and slid his finger inside her and she rippled at the sensation. He swore. "It's not enough. I want you every way at once."

He lowered his head to take her nipple into his mouth.

Adele arched toward him helplessly as he drove her mindless with his mouth and hands. His urgency fed hers. He made her reckless with need. She wanted closer. She wanted more of him. She squeezed his shoulders and slid her fingers down his smoothly muscled chest. He lifted his mouth from her breast to her lips.

"I want to kiss you everywhere," he said against her mouth.

Her need climbing, Adele skimmed her hands down his abdomen and brushed his hardness with her fingertips.

Jason stiffened. "Don't—"

Adele stroked him again and felt the first drops of his honeyed arousal. "Why—"

He swore and reached for protection. Her head spun with the speed. His gaze fastened on hers, he pushed her legs apart and plunged inside her.

Adele sucked in a sharp breath at the intimate invasion.

Jason closed his eyes and gritted his teeth. "You're so small."

She bit her lip. "And you are not," she said in a fractured whisper.

He laced the fingers of one of his hands through hers and gazed at her. "I don't want to hurt you."

"You didn't really hurt me," she said, slowly adjusting to him.

"No?" he said in disbelief.

"You just surprised me," she managed. "Kiss me," she said.

His eyes darkened with desire and, leaning down, he French kissed her mouth with caresses so hot she felt herself turn to liquid. He didn't move his lower body. He just made love to her mouth until Adele could stay still no longer.

"No," he told her.

But Adele didn't stop. She drew his tongue into her mouth as she undulated beneath him, swallowing his groan.

"You don't always follow instructions well," he said as he pulled back slightly, his face inches from hers, his eyes glittering.

"Aren't you glad?" She lifted her hand to his strong face and felt him sink into her more deeply.

Gazing down at her body, he began a mind-robbing rhythm, stretching her and pushing her with every stroke. Adele felt hot inside and out.

She arched against him, and he narrowed his eyes in pleasure. "I don't know how I'm going to get enough of you," he said and lowered his mouth to hers again.

The thrust of his tongue echoed the thrust of his masculinity inside her, and the sensations were too erotic for words. She felt herself tighten with each pump. Her breath shortened, and she felt herself drawn closer to the crest.

"C'mon, Addie, I want it all," he murmured in sensual encouragement. "I want all of you."

Like a tornado, it took her by surprise. She crested and clenched around him, feeling him stiffen with his own peak. Her climax rocked her to her core, and she clung to him, fearing she would splinter out of control.

Her mind a jumble of scrambled synapses, she tried to breathe and think. Jason rested his head in the hollow of her shoulder, his breaths as labored as hers. When Adele's brain began to operate, she was less concerned about her lungs and much more concerned about another, more vulnerable, part of her. She feared the man who had just taken her body had also taken her heart.

Jason wanted her again. The knowledge amazed him. He had never felt so sexually replete and hungry at the same time. His mind was already making love to her again, and he could feel his body react with shocking speed to the possibility.

Adele shifted beneath him, and he moved to her side to ease the burden of his weight from her, still keeping his arm around her waist. She tried to move away, and he instinctively tightened his arm and searched her face.

She looked lost.

His heart contracted at her expression. "What's wrong?"

She swallowed visibly. "I—uh—" She licked her lips. "I'm not used to this," she said in an unsteady voice.

He sat up, but didn't remove his hand from her. "To making love," he concluded. She'd been so incredibly tight.

"That, too," she said. "I—I'm not used to this."

He saw her hands tremble before she laced them together, and his heart caught again. Protective instincts rising to the surface, he pulled her into his lap, circling his arms around her. "Used to what?"

"To you," she said in a low voice. "To feeling like I got hit by a tornado."

"It was too fast," he said.

"No, no," she said, then looked up at him. "Was it?"

The artless trust in her gaze caught and held him. "Yes, it was," he said, lifting his hand to cup her jaw. When she rubbed her cheek against his palm, he felt the want like an ache, but not in his loins. "But I couldn't wait. It may not make sense to you, but I feel as though I've been waiting to make love to you since the moment I saw you." He paused. "And you?"

She lifted her gaze to his, and the power of the emotion in her eyes set him back. "Before," she finally said.

Confused, Jason dipped his head. "Before when?"

"Before I met you," she whispered, and rocked his world.

After that, Jason held her for the longest time, until Adele stopped trembling and relaxed in his arms. He woke her in the night and took her again like thunder and lightning. Then, with the dawn, he made love to her with such slow tenderness it made her tremble again.

So perhaps it had nothing to do with speed, she thought as she gingerly rose from her bed while he slept. Maybe the trembling was all because of him. The unsettling thought hovered over her while she performed the equally unsettling task of gathering her robe and Jason's clothes from her foyer. By the time she tied her robe and splashed her face with water, Adele had the foreboding sense that she had just made a whopper of a mistake.

Jason's hands around her waist took her by surprise, and she gave a little yelp. Completely at ease with his nudity, he lifted a dark eyebrow. "Jumpy this morning?"

"I guess," she said, and didn't like the indecisiveness of her answer. "Yes, I'm jumpy." She turned to face him. "I don't know how to do this."

"Do what?" he asked calmly.

"What we're doing," she said, flustered, and wondered if she'd ever been less articulate.

His lips twitched. "I'd say you've done a damn good job for a woman who doesn't know what she's doing."

She sighed in frustration. "That's not what I'm talking about. This is why I didn't want to do this," she said, knowing her articulation wasn't improving. "I mean, I'm not mistress material, and Heaven knows I'm not going to be your wife." Adele's heart felt as if it were clanging like an out-of-tune bell. *I don't even want to go near the wife thing,* she reminded herself. "But this is so intense. And there's your family."

"Let's leave my family out of this and keep what's private between us private," he said quietly. "I can take care of you."

His words chafed at her. "Can you? Can we? You may be your own man, but your family is a big part of you. How can they not see what's happening?"

His jaw tightened. "I've done it before."

Adele felt as if he'd slapped her. "Oh, you have? Gosh, I could have sworn you said this was different for you. But you've felt exactly this way before for another woman."

His eyes darkened with a hint of anger. "Adele," he began, impatience threading through his tone.

"I think you need to leave," she said.

"You misunderstood," he said.

"Yep, I think I did. You need to leave. I can't think with you standing naked less than a foot away from me. For that matter I can't think with you dressed in Eskimo wear twenty-five feet away from me. Please go.''

He wasn't budging. Her panic rose, and she knew she was going to have to do something drastic.

"I'm not leaving."

"Okay," she said. "You get dressed, and I'll go into the den."

He looked at her as if he didn't trust her, which was actually pretty darn smart of him. He glanced at her robe and probably drew the correct conclusion that she wasn't wearing a stitch beneath it. "Okay," he said reluctantly. "I'll be there in a minute."

He would be, but she would not, she thought as she grabbed her keys and a five-dollar bill from the kitchen. He must have heard her open the door. Just before she closed it behind her, she heard him yell.

"Adele!"

Eight

She was out of her league and out of her mind. "Let's keep our private life private." Adele echoed his words and made a sound of disgust. "Yeah, right. As if everyone who isn't blind won't be able to read my face every time I get within twenty-five feet of him."

Seeing the car in front of her pull away, she inched her car forward. The great thing about a fast-food breakfast was the drive-through window. Adele ordered seven items including two beverages, since she figured it would be a while before she returned home. She would be okay, she told herself. She had all her basic needs covered as well as her body. She had breakfast and a full tank of gas.

After she parked in the back of the parking lot,

far away from the road, she took a bite of a choles-
terol-laden egg, bacon and cheese biscuit and sipped
her orange juice.

Okay, so maybe it wasn't the most rational move
in the world to walk out of her condo with no shoes
and covered only in a thin wash of silk. It couldn't
be any less rational than going to bed with Jason
Fortune last night.

She took another bite of the biscuit and scowled.
It must be nice to have that much self-control. Once
upon a time she'd had that kind of self-control.

She crumpled the paper around the biscuit and
reached for the hash browns. "I do not like this. I
do not like this," she repeated like a litany to herself.

Adele traded the juice for coffee and took a long
swallow of the strong, hot liquid. She took another
sip and forced her brain out of neutral.

Jason might wait at her house for a while, but
since he was Mr. Very Important to Fortune Construction, he couldn't dawdle too long on Monday
morning. Adele thought of the recent accident, and
her appetite left her. She tossed the hash browns
back in the bag.

Sighing, she decided she would face the big bad
Fortune lion later after she'd gathered her compo-
sure. Fast food, a shower and a very tight hair clip
would help her project outward calm.

By the time Jason reached the office, he wanted
to chew glass. As he passed his assistant, he barked

out an instruction, "Barbara, page me the second Miss O'Neil arrives."

"Yes, sir," she said. "There are messages and your brother—"

Jason opened the door to Tyler.

"Your brother is here needing to kill time until the safety inspection clears us to start construction again."

Jason took a deep breath and understood his brother's inability to remain idle. The events of the previous days had the potential to drive any man to the edge. Speaking of driving a man to the edge, he thought, and his mind traveled to the red-haired witch who had abandoned him this morning.

"You can set up preliminary plans for the Westin project in Rio," Jason said, closing the door behind him.

"I thought that was a maybe," Tyler said.

"It became a yes last week."

Tyler shrugged. "That's why you're vice president of marketing. If anyone can turn a no or maybe into a yes, it's you."

Jason again thought of Adele and bit his tongue.

Tyler scrutinized him, his gaze lingering on the places where Jason had cut himself shaving. "You don't look too good. Did you have a rough night?"

"I'm okay. My morning just wasn't smooth as glass."

Tyler tensed. "Did one of the investigators call with bad news?"

Jason shook his head. "No. Nothing like that."

Tyler crinkled his face in confusion. "Then

what—'' He broke off and studied Jason. "Something to do with the redhead wonder?''

Jason paused a half beat too long. He knew it by the expression of realization on Tyler's face. "Did you finally get her into bed?''

Irritation flooded him. "It's not like that,'' he told Tyler. "You asked for something to do. Get out of here and work on the Westin project.''

"Let me guess. You spent the night with her, and she wants to get married now.''

"Not exactly,'' Jason said. "She walked out on me this morning,'' he said, still incredulous.

Tyler shrugged. "That happens sometimes. Women are weird. Maybe she wasn't comfortable at your house or something.''

"We weren't at my house,'' Jason said.

"Huh?'' Tyler said. "Well, where were you?''

"At the condo. She started this insane conversation, told me to leave, then when I wouldn't, she sneaked out the door while I was getting dressed. She wasn't wearing a damn thing beneath that robe,'' he muttered to himself, pacing.

Tyler began to chuckle. "She ran out on you from the condo, which is technically her house while she is here?'' He laughed again. "That's desperate, Jason. What did you do to the poor woman?''

Tyler remembered their lovemaking and slowed his pacing. "Nothing to make her leave. Nothing—'' He broke off and scowled. "When she gets in here, I'm giving her a short course in etiquette if I don't wring her neck first.''

Tyler nodded slowly. "Oh, well, that should make her come running."

Jason's temper flared. "This is none of your business. I don't want you discussing it with anyone, especially Mom or Dad."

"You really think Dad won't be able to tell? He can read either of us like a book."

"I don't care. I don't want you discussing it. I don't encourage Mom and Dad to force matrimony down your throat, and believe me, the opportunity presents on a regular basis."

"Okay, okay," Tyler said, raising his fingers in the sign of the cross.

Jason pulled the Westin file from a drawer and handed it to Tyler. "Knock yourself out."

Tyler nodded. "I will," he said. "Good luck with the redhead."

The redhead arrived when Jason was on a conference call. As soon as he concluded it, he took a deep breath and walked to Adele's office. Her door barely ajar, she sat behind her desk reading a professional journal and making notes. Her hair was pulled back more tightly than usual and she wore black. *Don't mess with me.* Too late, he thought, and pushed open the door.

She looked up, and her eyes flashed with turbulent emotion. Everything about her seemed on guard. She stood. "I'm sorry I left so abruptly this morning, but I'm not sorry, too."

Jason's head began to pound. "We couldn't accomplish anything by your leaving."

"Actually I did. I ate a fast-food breakfast and worked on regaining my sanity."

"And did you succeed?"

The vulnerability in her gaze tugged at him. "I started in that direction." She inhaled and looked away. "I know it wasn't wise for us to get involved."

Jason felt his gut twist. "If you could turn back time, would you make a different choice?"

She closed her eyes and was silent for a long moment. "No, but it's not going to work. You may be able to hide your emotions, but I just don't have that talent."

Jason walked behind and closed his arms around her. "Maybe we shouldn't hide it."

Adele turned in his arms and looked at him as if he were crazy. "And you think Kate Fortune, your mother or your father will have nothing to say or suggest? You know what Kate is like. She'll have the flowers picked out for our fictitious wedding before you or I can scream help."

Jason grimaced. She had a point, but he was determined to continue seeing her. The prospect of not holding her, not knowing her was like barbed wire on his nerve endings. "You don't really think we can go back, do you?"

She frowned. "I don't know. I just know I'm not mistress or wife material, so what does that make me?"

"How about lover, friend and disruptive force in my life?"

She gave him a thoughtful glance. "Maybe," she

said with grudging approval. "And how do we respond to questions?"

"We don't," he said, and smiled. "We change the subject or flat-out say we're not discussing the matter."

Adele looked doubtful. "Do you really think that will work?"

Jason pushed her door closed, locked it and drew her into his arms. "I don't want you to think about Kate Fortune or my mother or father or any other Fortunes right now." He brushed his lips against hers and felt his body buzz with the memory of their intimacy. "I want you to think about me," he said, and did his best to wipe everything else from her mind.

Much later he found her in her office again.

"I'll take you to dinner tonight," Jason said after he had finished an extensive international project meeting. Between the aftermath of the accident and new accounts, he'd had to ask Adele to go ahead with preliminary proposals for some of the hospital policy. Her hair escaping the topknot and her feet shoeless, she sat in a chair beside her desk with her feet propped up on a small cabinet. She didn't appear nearly so stiff and distant as she had earlier today. Looking at her made him ache and feel soothed at the same time. Damn combination, he thought.

She shook her head. "I don't think so." She wrinkled her nose. "I'm not ready for a public appearance."

Her rejection caught him off guard. Jason had

spent his life being pursued by women who'd been far more interested in his name, his money and the prestige of being associated with him. "Are you saying you don't want to be seen with me?"

She gave a lop-sided smile. "Pretty much." She swung her legs around and stood. "You can come to my condo for dinner if you like, though."

He wanted more than anything to understand her. "I thought you didn't want to be a mistress."

"I'm not. I'm just not ready to be referred to as Jason Fortune's woman *du jour*."

He rolled his eyes. "You're getting me confused with Tyler again."

She met his gaze, and her expression turned serious. "Not a chance."

He relented, but in an odd way her reluctance bothered him. Jason couldn't explain it, but he was torn between hiding Adele and what they shared away from prying eyes and staking his claim in public. He felt a disconcerting possessiveness about her, and if Adele knew, she was so damned independent he was certain she'd be horrified.

She prepared a stir-fry that they didn't quite finish before he made love to her. Afterward, she was cold, so he wrapped a blanket around them both and sat up to hold her. He lifted her bare fingers to his lips and kissed them. "Why don't you wear jewelry?"

"I wear earrings every once in a while."

"But no rings," he said, then skimmed his finger over her neck. "No necklace."

"When I was pretty young, I had a roommate named Annabelle at the children's home for almost two years. She kept insisting that her mother was going to come and take her away after she got well. That was everyone's dream, so one really believed her." She smiled. "Except me. I knew about Annabelle's stuff."

"Stuff," he echoed, intrigued.

"Annabelle had jewelry. She had a ring with her birthstone and a bracelet with her name engraved on it. She wore a locket around her neck with teeny, tiny pictures of Annabelle and her mother inside it. When she wasn't wearing her jewelry she kept it in a music box." A look of bittersweet reminiscence crossed Adele's features.

"Some of the other girls were jealous of Annabelle's stuff. It was pretty, but I never wanted her stuff as much as I wanted the stories that went with them. Annabelle's mother put the ring in a birthday cupcake for Annabelle's sixth birthday."

Adele smiled. "The bracelet had a secret message on the inside. I L Y, Mom. And the coolest thing of all was the music box. It played 'Edelweiss,' which is a very pretty song. But what made it special was that Annabelle's mother used to sing 'Edelweiss' to her every night when she put her to bed."

"Did her mother ever come for her?" Jason asked, lacing his fingers through Adele's hair.

Adele nodded. "Yes. Annabelle's mother had gotten tuberculosis, and it took a long time for her to get well, but when she did, she came and got Annabelle. I'd never seen people so happy they cried. I was sad that she left, but I couldn't be real sad because they were so happy. So I think Annabelle shaped my attitude about jewelry.''

"How?"

"If I'm going to wear jewelry, I want a story to go with it. Otherwise, it's just stuff.''

Moved, he said nothing, but tucked her head beneath his chin. Jason thought of Cara and how important jewelry had been to her. The flashier the diamond, the better. Sometimes, perhaps most of the time, he had sensed his family's wealth and name had been more important to his wife than he had been. He thought of Adele as a child and all she must have longed for. His heart hurt, and he felt a powerful, driving urge to give her everything she'd never had, everything she should have had. The urge was so strong it disturbed him. He wasn't ready to care so much.

With each question answered about her, however, two new questions grew in its place. Where, he wondered, would it end?

The following day Adele tried to adjust to the sense of being off-kilter. Her heart didn't beat the same way it did before. "Maybe I need a pacemaker," she muttered to herself as she sat in his office while he finished a telephone call with someone on the other side of the world. Jason Fortune had messed up her orderly existence. For Adele it was a matter of choosing between two evils, and Jason was too compelling to pass up.

They'd spent the morning making fast headway on plans for the outpatient teen pregnancy center.

She admired his ability to see the big picture and at the same time to pay attention to details. Gazing surreptitiously at him, she took in the easy way he wore a suit and remembered the equally easy way he wore nothing. He was handsome in a way that would always turn women's head, but what held Adele's attention was the way his mind and heart worked.

She glanced down at the framed picture of Lisa and smiled.

Jason hung up the phone and checked his watch. "Where were we?"

"At a good stopping place," Adele said. "How did Lisa's slumber party go?"

"She had a good time, and my mother has spoiled her to death during the past few days. Last night was her first night back. That's why I didn't stay late last night," he said. "She asked about you."

Adele felt a rush of pleasure. "Really? I was just thinking I've missed seeing her."

He nodded, but said nothing.

Adele studied his face and sensed something wasn't quite right. "Are you sure she's okay? Are you worried about her?"

He sighed and raked his hand through his hair. "She's fine. I haven't decided how to handle her and you."

"Her and me?" Adele asked, confused.

"She hasn't really had a mother figure in her life except for her grandmother, and she's very impressed with you."

Adele would have felt flattered except Jason didn't sound pleased. "Is that a problem?"

"I don't know. I'm concerned that she may get attached to you."

Her stomach gave a vicious twist. His words emphasized the temporary nature of their relationship. That should be fine, Adele told herself. Neither of them wanted anything permanent. They weren't suited for anything permanent.

"Your job here will be done as soon as you and I complete the operations for the hospital," he said, and Adele could tell he was reading her face.

Darn, she wished she were better at hiding her emotions. She bit her lip. "I understand that you would want a more permanent feminine influence on your daughter," she said.

He rounded his desk to stand in front of her. "She's so young, and it may not make sense, but I want to protect her from any more loss as much as I can."

Adele understood his need to protect. She wished she understood why it hurt so much. "You weren't worried about this the first night you had me over to dinner."

He shook his head. "I had no idea how quickly she would grow attached to you."

Or how quickly Adele would grow attached to Lisa, she thought, struggling with her feelings.

"This isn't anything personal," he said. "I just need—"

Adele lifted her hand. "I understand. It's a good thing for you to protect your daughter," she said, because although it hurt, it was the right thing to say. Clearing her throat, she glanced down and caught sight of her watch. "I hate to remind you, but it's probably time to leave for Mike Dodd's funeral."

He nodded slowly. "Can I give you a ride?"

"I'll drive myself," she said, needing to pull back into herself a bit.

He reached out for her hand. "I don't want you to be hurt by this. I would rather hurt myself."

Adele felt her eyes grow damp and blinked to keep telltale tears at bay. She could hear his desire to protect her and his daughter tearing at him.

Even though she missed Lisa and would have loved to know her better, Adele was deeply touched that Jason so wanted not to hurt her. Somewhere inside her, she found the strength that had gotten her through similar times, times when she'd felt as if she'd been on the outside looking in.

"There's no need to hurt yourself. I'm okay," she said, and if it wasn't true at the moment, she would make it true. "We need to leave."

In her car, she followed Jason to the memorial service at the small chapel. Sitting in the back, she watched Jason and Tyler speak to a young woman whose face looked strained with grief. Angelica Dodd, Mike's sister. She felt a well of sympathy for the woman. Adele had been told Angelica and Mike had no other family, so Angelica was now alone.

Adele saw several men with the trademark Fortune bone structure and was impressed by the presence of them at the service. In particular, Riley Fortune, hovered by Angelica's side.

The minister began the service with prayer and scripture, then shared a message about the fleeting, uncertain nature of life, and the importance of living life to the fullest while we can, the importance of loving to the fullest while we can.

Adele's heart tightened and she studied Jason's profile. She had never loved a man before, but he was taking her to places she'd never been, teaching her things about herself she'd never known. Her biggest fear was that she would learn she wasn't nearly so strong and independent as she'd believed, because when it was all said and done, Adele was certain she would be alone again. She was not a keeper.

Nine

"**D**addy, who was the man that died?" Lisa asked as Jason tucked her into one of the guest room beds at his parents' home. Jason had decided that staying with his parents a few extra days would offer an extra boost of security during the crisis.

"He was a foreman," Jason told her, brushing her hair from her face.

"Why did he die?"

His daughter was always full of questions, particularly at bedtime. "The elevator broke."

"Is it fixed?"

"By the end of the week it will be." He touched his forefinger to her nose. "It's time for you to go to sleep. You have school tomorrow."

Lisa sat up. "But I haven't shown you the bracelets I'm making yet."

Jason knew she was stalling, but he didn't mind giving her extra attention, especially with all the disruptions lately. Although he had wanted to see Adele after the memorial service, Jason had known he needed to spend some time with Lisa. "Okay," he said, "show me."

Lisa leaned over and pulled two beaded bracelets from a pocket of her backpack beside the bed. "My teacher helped me get started. See the colors," she said. "Green, red, black and amber." She looked up at him proudly. "Guess why I picked those colors."

Her enthusiasm warmed him. He smiled. "You got me. Why?"

"Because Adele's eyes are green, her hair is red, my hair is black, and my eyes are amber. I want to give her one to thank her for rescuing me."

Jason's heart twisted. He was proud of his daughter for her attitude of gratitude and generosity, but it was easy to see Lisa was already attached. He put his arm around her. "Princess, the bracelets are very pretty and it's very very nice of you to make one for Adele. You do understand that she's not moving permanently to Pueblo. She's doing a special job for the hospital, and then she'll go back to Minnesota." Stating the fact brought him no joy.

Lisa wrinkled her brow in confusion. "Do I have time to give her the bracelet before she leaves? Is she leaving tomorrow?"

"She's not leaving tomorrow. It will probably be in a few months."

Lisa's face brightened. "Then I've got plenty of time to give it to her, and when she goes back to

Minnesota and looks at her bracelet, she can think of me.'' She paused. ''Do you think she would wear it?''

Jason thought of how Adele would respond to the small gift. ''Yeah, I think she would.'' He brushed his lips over her small cheek, and she reached up to squeeze his neck.

His mind busy, he softly closed the door behind him and walked toward the den. His mother sat on the leather couch reading a book. She glanced up.

''Where's Dad?'' Jason asked.

She cocked her head toward the outdoor patio. ''Outside,'' she said with a soft smile. ''You know how he loves the rain.''

Jason stepped through the sliding door and watched the proud outline of his father as he stood in the backyard in the rain. His father was an intriguing mix of Papago and Fortune. He'd graduated near the top of his class in college, yet there'd always been a spiritual quality to him. His father had often said Jason had inherited that same quality, but Jason didn't see it in himself.

He thought of the many times throughout his growing-up years when he'd followed his father out into the rain and learned to enjoy the rare moisture. It had been a while, but tonight was no different from many other times. He walked toward his father and felt the cool rain on his skin.

''Feels good,'' Devlin said.

''A little chilly,'' Jason said wryly. ''It's February.''

Devlin gave a slight grin. ''You're bothered.''

Jason knew it was useless to deny it. "About several things."

Devlin sighed. "The accident. Everyone at Fortune is bothered about it. But you're bothered about the woman."

Jason noticed he didn't say *a* woman. He said *the* woman, as if it were a foregone conclusion he was speaking of Adele. "Lisa is growing attached to her too quickly. She'll be hurt when Adele leaves."

"Probably," Devlin said.

Jason waited for his father to expound, but he didn't. "So?" he prompted.

"So, like the rain, good people and bad people come and go in our lives. Would you give up the benefit you receive from a rain shower because it might be a long time before the rain returns?"

His father's wisdom was simple and right, as usual. Jason turned his head up to the sky and reveled in the sensation of the cool rain on his face. "When did you get to be so smart?"

"When you turned twenty-five," Devlin said with a hint of humor in his voice. "All children believe their fathers are ignorant until they grow out of their teen years."

Adele saw very little of Jason on Wednesday. Between new contracts and keeping a close eye on the progressing investigation, his plate was full. She struggled with how much she missed him. It had only been a day, she told herself. How silly, she thought. It wasn't as if he were oxygen and she needed him to breathe.

Adele repeated that to herself throughout the day and evening, but when she fell asleep, she dreamed of Jason. She awakened to the sound of her doorbell ringing. Adele squinted at her alarm clock. Just after 6 a.m. Who!

Dragging herself out of bed, she shoved her arms through the sleeves of her robe and looked through the peephole. Jason. Her heart jumped.

She opened the door. "What in the world—"

"Quick," he said, carrying a small box. "Name your favorite childhood movie."

Her brain still in bed, Adele shrugged. "Uh, *Willie Wonka and the Chocolate Factory*."

Jason shook his head in pity. "Try again."

"Uh, *Snow White*."

He sighed. "One more. A classic."

She closed her eyes to concentrate, but the faint teasing scent of his aftershave distracted her. *"Wizard of Oz,"* she said.

"You win," he said, and gave her the box.

"What is it?" she asked, confused, but filled with a crazy delight.

"Open it and find out," he told her, and reached out to touch her hair. "I love your hair like this."

Adele shuddered at her mental image. "Oh, God, I can imagine what it looks like. Think Wicked Witch."

"Think Rapunzel or Goldilocks in red," he said.

Adele felt a soft spot expanding inside her. She could get used to hearing things like that, she warned herself, and turned her attention to the box. She pulled out a porcelain music box with a painted rainbow, a pot of gold and birds and flowers. She twisted it and listened to the familiar lovely tune. "'Somewhere over the Rainbow.' Why?" she asked, touched.

"You've had a lot of rain in your life, but you live your life as if you are a rainbow." He shoved his hands in his pockets as if he were uncomfortable. "Corny, but true."

Her heart felt as if it would burst. Adele's eyes filled with tears, and she turned away to quickly swipe at them. "I've been called a lot of things in my life, but no one has ever called me a rainbow." Taking a deep breath, she tried to collect herself. "Well," she said brightly, turning back to face him. "Are you going to sing it for me?"

Jason blinked. "What?"

"The song," she said, pointing to the music box.

"Adele," he said with a mock-serious expression on his face as he pulled her into his arms, "I never want to hurt you that way."

She laughed despite the fact that she was still so moved she almost didn't know what to say. She buried her face against the fine cotton shirt that covered his chest. "Thank you for giving me a story."

Adele felt like a kid about that music box. She took it with her to work so she could look at it throughout the day. She resisted the urge to show everyone the music box by cherishing her secret story. She smiled every time she looked at it.

It was a keeper, she thought, but that didn't mean she was a keeper for Jason. Adele decided that insane whisper of possibility was the biggest danger,

the most seductive lie she might fall into believing.
Yes, she had fallen for him, but she must never ever
lose sight of the fact that this was temporary. She
wasn't Cinderella. She didn't have a fairy god-
mother. And when it was all over, she didn't want
to turn into a pumpkin.

"Hi, there, rainbow," said the man who turned
her brain to mush.

Adele glanced up and smiled.

"Something's different," he said with a teasing
glint in his eye as he looked around the room. "I
can't put my finger on it."

Adele felt her smile grow. "Like heck you
can't!"

"You brought it to the office?"

She stood and lifted her shoulders. "It makes me
feel good to look at it."

"Good," he said, moving closer to her and cap-
turing her gaze. "Tell me how to make you feel
good by looking at me."

"You make me feel lots of things," she said as
he lowered his mouth and barely brushed his lips
against hers. Her heart rate picked up.

"What things?" he prompted, dragging his mouth
over hers again, teasing her with the promise of
more.

"Hot," she said, and saw her passion reflected in
his eyes.

"And?" He lowered his hands to her waist and
drew her closer.

"Excited, a little scared, very crazy, and—" She
broke off, feeling self-conscious.

"And what?" He searched her gaze, then nuzzled her cheek. "Tell me."

Adele closed her eyes. As if she could refuse him, she thought. "You make me feel soft," she said in a low voice, "inside."

His arms tightened slightly around her, and Adele felt something rare and new to her: tenderness. She savored the surprise and wonder of it for a full moment. Safety, warmth, almost love. She gulped.

"You also make me feel hungry," she said.

"Good, then you can join me at the Camel Corral for dinner tonight," he said smoothly.

The invitation jolted Adele. She pulled back slightly. "Did I say hungry? Maybe I meant another word."

"You said hungry," he assured her. "Best steak dinner in town."

"Did I ever tell you I was a vegetarian?"

"No, because you're not."

Damn, the man was too smart. "I could fix a nice—"

"I want to take you out." He put his thumb under her chin and nudged her gaze upward to meet his. "Why don't you want to go out with me?"

"It's not that I don't want to go out with you. I just don't want to deal with the whispers or the comments. It's so wonderful when it's just you and me." She wrinkled her nose. "I don't want to contaminate it."

"There will be no contamination," he told her. "Quit stalling."

At Jason's insistence, Adele traveled in his Jaguar

to the popular steakhouse on Four Corners Crossing. She stepped across richly patterned, mosaic-tiled floors to a booth across from the nonworking fireplace. A chunky candle lit the darkly masculine table.

"Very nice," she said, "but I don't think my music box would have fit in here."

He gave a sexy grin. "I'm glad you like it."

"I do," she said. "What should I order for dinner?"

"Steak or prime rib." He glanced around.

"Are you looking for something?"

He shook his head. "I just remembered that Mike Dodd's sister, Angelica, works here. There's been a lot of talk about how Riley has been very diligent in his efforts to comfort Angelica."

"Is that something to worry about?"

He rubbed his chin. "I don't know. You know me and questions."

"You like them answered."

"Yes," he said, and his gaze focused on her. "All of them. Any contamination?"

"No," she admitted. "And we won't even have to worry about the dishes."

The waitress appeared, and they placed their orders. Adele relaxed and enjoyed their conversation. His appeal and undivided attention were habit forming. Something about the way he looked at her made her feel as if he was making love to her with his eyes, and she found it difficult to look away.

"I want to make love to you," he told her.

"I know," she said.

His gaze darkened, and he swore under his breath. "If this were a hotel, I'd have you upstairs within seconds."

"I guess that's the advantage of eating in."

He shook his head and chuckled at her.

"Jason," a woman's voice broke in. "It's been ages."

Adele tore her gaze from his and glanced up at the tall, cool blonde standing by the table. Adele immediately sensed that Jason's relationship with this woman had been more than casual. Her stomach gave an involuntary twist. She felt Jason's gaze on her as he stood.

"This is Adele O'Neil," he said, and nodded a bit stiffly. "Colleen Johnson."

Adele extended her hand and murmured. "So nice to meet you."

"And you," Colleen said. "Are you new to town? I don't recall seeing you before."

"I haven't been in Pueblo very long. I'm working with Jason to set up some parameters for the Children's Hospital."

"Oh," she said, giving Adele an assessing glance. "The Children's Hospital. I've told Jason it's a wonderful thing his family is doing." She turned to Jason and smiled. "I've missed you. Call me."

Then Colleen walked away, leaving a trail of perfume and an unpleasant taste in Adele's mouth.

Jason sat down and met Adele's gaze. "It's in the past," he told her.

He didn't deny that he and Colleen had been lovers. Adele's stomach twisted again. "She wishes it weren't past."

"Probably," he said with a shrug and a cynical lift to his lips. "She has a deep affection for my last name and what it means at the local bank."

Adele rolled her eyes. "You underestimate your appeal. If your last name were Smith or Jones, you would still be a strong, dynamic man who inspired interest, admiration and—" she leaned forward "—lust."

His eyes lit like twin flames, and he reached for her hand. "That kind of talk could get you into trouble," he said.

Adele's heart flipped. "I think I'm safe in public. You're a discreet man."

"Don't push me."

And she suddenly wanted to do the exact opposite. She tugged their joined hands to her mouth. "Why, Mr. Smith, you wouldn't be threatening me, would you?"

"Not threatening. Warning," he said, watching her carefully.

"Sounds like a dare, Mr. Smith," she said, and followed a dark little impulse. She skimmed her tongue over his finger.

Jason stiffened. "I warned you," he said in a quiet voice, then quickly stood and pulled her with him before she could blink.

Her heart stuttered. He wore the same expression on his face as when he made love to her. "We haven't paid the check."

"They can put it on my tab," he told her, and led

her to his car. As soon as he shut the door, he pulled her into his arms and gave her a French kiss that took her around the world and back.

If she were the type to swoon, she would be swooning right now. Her head, however, only *seemed* to be moving in a circle, she told herself and took a deep breath. She just needed oxygen. Lots of it. Her lips buzzed, her breasts were swollen, she was shockingly aroused. "Does this mean I should stop calling you Mr. Smith?"

Jason gave a rough chuckle and started the engine. "That won't stop me."

He drove her home and reached for her as soon as he parked the car in the parking lot. "I can't stay tonight," he said regretfully. "I need to get home to Lisa."

A sense of urgency hung thickly in the air between them. "I want you," he said in a voice that was nearly a growl. He consumed her mouth, and she could feel his hunger. His breath came fast and short like hers. The muscles of his arms flexed beneath her touch. She could drown in the taste of him. He made her feel as if she were on fire all over. Her breasts brushed against his chest, and she made a sound of frustration at her inability to get closer.

"What's wrong?" he asked.

"You're too far away," she said.

He groaned and pushed his seat all the way back, then pulled her onto his lap. She straddled him while he ate at her mouth. He loosened her hair and skimmed his hands down to her hips, rocking her against his hardness. It was a carnal, sensual move that made her weak with wanting.

He slid his hands up her bare thighs. Adele trembled. "What are we doing?" The need in her voice took her by surprise.

"I have protection," he said, sliding his hands beneath her panties. He looked at her through hooded lids as if she were the most important woman in the world to him, and at that moment, Adele would have given him anything.

She swallowed hard. "Why do you have protection?"

"I always carry protection when I'm around you," he said in a tone that was so darkly wry it was sexy. "I've thought about taking you on my desk too many times to count."

Excitement coursed through her. "We're in a car," she whispered.

Jason touched her intimately and found her wet and swollen. He stroked and fondled her. "Have you ever done it in a car?"

"No," she said, trying not to shudder.

"Have you ever wanted to?" he asked her, rubbing his open mouth against hers.

Adele shuddered despite herself. "No."

His fingers continued their lazy, seductive trail of mass destruction on her nerve endings. "Do you want to now?"

Adele knew he would stop if she asked. But she didn't want him to. "Yes," she whispered, and the next sound she heard was the rip of her panties.

Ten

Early the following morning, Adele awakened to a tapping sound at the back of her condo unit. She frowned and squinted her eyes. Promptly closing them when she saw it wasn't quite dawn, she rubbed her face into her pillow.

The tapping continued, louder.

Adele groaned. "Woodpeckers in Arizona?" She covered her head with her pillow. She needed her sleep. After last night— Her face heated at the thought of it. She couldn't believe her wantonness. *In the car.*

After they had taken each other with a wildness she'd never even dreamed, he'd walked her to her door. His tenderness and reluctance to leave her had further weakened her knees and softened a heart that had already melted.

Adele sighed, remembering. The tapping penetrated the delicious fog of her memory. Swearing, she tossed her pillow against the wall, snatched up her robe and punched her arms through the sleeves as she stomped downstairs. She jerked open the curtains to her patio door and found Jason staring back at her. Her heart bumped against her rib cage.

"What are you doing?" she asked.

"Open the door," he mouthed.

Confused, she did, and immediately heard the tinkling sound of her music box. "You left it in my car," he said. "I'm going out of town for a few days, and I didn't want you to be without it."

Adele felt torn—touched that he had brought the music box to her and upset that he was leaving. "Thank you," she said, wrapping her arms around herself in the cool morning air as the sun rose over the horizon. "Where are you going?"

"L.A. I'm meeting an international client there." He pulled her against him. "Will you miss me?"

She pressed her face into his chest and inhaled his scent. "I already do," she confessed.

"I'm not crazy about leaving right now, either," he said, and wrapped one of his hands around her, then guided her into a slow semidance on the small patio.

"What are you doing?" she asked.

"Dancing with you before I leave. Wouldn't want you to forget me," he said with a slight grin, as if it were the most natural thing in the world to dance with her at dawn. As if it were possible for her to forget him.

Fat chance.

"Reserve Valentine's evening for me. Kate is having a little gathering. My family will be there, including Lisa."

"Are you sure it's a good idea for me to join you?" she asked, remembering his earlier reservations.

"Yes. Lisa has a small gift she wants to give you."

"I thought you didn't want her to get attached to me."

"What am I supposed to say to her? Do as I say, not as I do?"

Adele's chest grew tight, but she refused to allow herself to believe he was growing attached to her. "You're not getting attached to me."

"Oh?" he said. "Then what am I doing?"

"You're temporarily intrigued."

He met her gaze. "Now who's underestimating?"

"Overestimating some things can be very dangerous," she murmured, reminding herself not to grow accustomed to the way Jason's arms felt around her. She deliberately lightened the mood. "Have fun in the land of smog."

He gave her a look of mock disapproval. "If you were mine, I would require you to go with me."

If you were mine. Adele's heart jumped. Erase it, she told herself. Forget he said it. Pretend you didn't hear it. She forced a smile and lifted her chin. "You really seem to get into giving orders a bit much, Your Highness."

"Would you go with me?" he challenged.

"Maybe," she said. In a heartbeat. "If you asked very nicely."

He growled and lifted her feet off the ground, high in the air, so that she looked down at him.

"Put me down!"

"Maybe," he said, slowly skimming her down the front of him, inch by mesmerizing inch. He halted when her mouth was a breath from his. "If you ask very nicely."

Adele didn't see any way out, so she kissed him. It occurred to her that Jason Fortune was far more dangerous than she'd predicted; not because of his power or his wealth, not because he gave her stuff, but because he gave her memories.

Five days later Adele nervously prepared for her date with Jason. She'd changed dresses three times, her hair had a mind of its own and she'd poked a hole through a fresh pair of stockings. She wasn't just nervous about seeing Jason for the first time since he'd been away. She wasn't just nervous about appearing with him in front of his family.

She was nervous because she was late.

It didn't mean anything, she told herself. Just because Colorado could have set the atomic clock, the most precise clock in the world, by her menstrual cycle, it didn't mean she was pregnant. They'd used protection every time. She was certain. There'd been that one dreamy coupling in the middle of the night, but both she and Jason were so conscientious about protection that she knew he had used protection. She couldn't be pregnant. Her cycle was just a little haywire because she'd fallen in love. Panic sliced through her.

"Damn!" she said and poked her nail through her last pair of stockings. "It's not love," she told herself. "It's gratitude. It's respect, fascination, desire—" She fought the urge to cry. "Oh, I can't fall in love with him. It would be so stupid."

Taking a deep breath, she closed her eyes. She wasn't pregnant. She had a doctor's appointment tomorrow to start birth control pills. It would all be settled tomorrow.

The doorbell rang. Her heart jumped. She opened her eyes, stared into the mirror and saw a woman in love. "Stop it," she hissed, and rushed toward the door. Even though Jason had called her several times when he'd been away, she'd wondered if he would feel the same way for her when he returned.

Pulling the door open, she drank in the sight of the man who had haunted every other thought her brain had formed during the past few days. Dressed in a casual, Western-style suit and wearing an intent gaze that warmed her to her toes, he stole her breath.

"Hi," he said.

She felt his gaze skim over her, taking in her short-sleeve, burgundy velvet sheath, her wild hair that she'd worn loose for him and lingering on her lips. "I'm half tempted to forget the party and keep you to myself tonight, but Lisa would kill me."

He leaned down to kiss her. "Damn you, you bothered me even while I was gone."

"Then we're even," Adele said. She saw something in his eyes, something more than fleeting passion that alternately frightened and thrilled her. Afraid of how much it meant to her, she pulled back.

He cocked his head to one side. "Edgy?" he asked.

She nodded.

"The party?"

The party, my period is late, I love you and want you to love me. Adele just bit her lip and nodded.

"Don't worry," he said, leading her to his car. "If they start putting bamboo shoots under your fingernails, I'll take you away."

"I feel so much better," she said wryly.

He stopped directly in front of her before he opened her car door. "We won't stay long. I have other plans."

Adele couldn't tell whether that made her feel relieved or more nervous. As soon as they arrived at Kate's home, she and Jason were pulled in different directions.

Kate welcomed her and directed her to a table laden with finger foods and desserts. Adele couldn't have been less hungry, but she nibbled on a couple of crackers.

Tyler appeared by her side. "Great spread."

"It's beautiful," she said. "How are you?"

"The preliminary safety report is complete, and the service elevator has been repaired, so we've been given the green light to continue construction." Concern flickered across his face. "We've beefed up security." He grabbed some caviar and a cracker. "Where's your date?"

Adele caught sight of Jason across the room. As

if he sensed her, he glanced up and met her gaze. Her heart fluttered. "Someone snagged him as soon as we came in the door. I think it might be a local politician."

Tyler glanced up and nodded. "Yep, the mayor."

"Where's your date?" she asked.

He shook his head. "Don't have one."

"It's interesting the way I keep hearing that you have this reputation with the ladies, but I've yet to see a date by your side."

He shot her a cagey glance. "I work very hard to cultivate that reputation."

"It's all done with smoke and mirrors, isn't it?"

Tyler looked down his nose at her in an expression vaguely reminiscent of Jason when he was displeased. "My brother told me you're entirely too smart."

She smiled. "Your brother is just used to getting his way."

"True," he said and nodded. "But don't let him fool you. He's one of those guys who makes it all look easy. But everything hasn't been easy for him."

Adele wanted to ask Tyler what he meant, but someone chose that moment to clang a spoon against a wineglass. Adele craned her neck to spy the mirror image of Devlin Fortune trying to get everyone's attention. "Is that your father's brother?" she whispered.

"Hunter," he said with a nod.

Hunter cleared his throat and smiled down at an exquisite young woman with raven hair and violet eyes and a tall, pleased-looking man standing beside her. "I'm happy to announce the engagement of my daughter, Isabelle, to Brad Rowan. Please join me in congratulating them."

The guests burst into applause, and Adele glanced once again across the room at Jason. For a moment her wayward mind conjured a forbidden picture. She had not permitted herself to visualize a future with Jason, but what if something magical and amazing happened and they were meant to be forever? What if she and Jason were to marry? What if he became her husband? And she his wife? Adele felt her chest swell at the thought. Waking up with him every morning, sharing the happiness and the difficulties and all the love.

What would it be like, she wondered, to be Jason's love? To be the woman he turned to for the rest of his life. The image filled her with such a sense of completeness it sent her spinning.

"Adele, Adele, I made something for you," Lisa said, tugging at her arm and pulling her away from her seductive daydream.

"Your father told me you were going to give me a gift."

Lisa's face fell. "Did he blab and tell you what it was?"

Adele laughed. "No. I'm dying of curiosity."

Lisa tugged her away from the crowd, and they sat together on a small overstuffed love seat. "I wanted to give you a gift for saving me from the bike accident," Lisa said.

"Oh, sweetie, you didn't have to do that."

"But I wanted to," she said earnestly, and pulled two bracelets from a small cloth purse. "I got some help from my teacher, and I made you and me bracelets. The beads are green and red and black and amber. Green and red for your eyes and hair, and black and amber for my hair and eyes."

Too moved for words, Adele shook her head and felt tears threaten. She took Lisa in her arms and hugged her tightly.

"Don't you like it?" Lisa asked uncertainly.

Adele felt a tear sneak down her cheek. "Oh, it's the nicest thing anyone has every made for me."

"It is?" Lisa asked, and Adele could see the confusion because of the life of privilege Lisa had lived.

"Yes, it is," Adele said, sniffing. "And I want to put it on right now."

"It's not as fancy as diamonds," Lisa told her.

"Oh, sweetheart, it's a million times better than diamonds," Adele insisted, and hugged Lisa again. "Thank you." She sat with Lisa for several more moments, and the two of them discussed school and softball.

"Y'know," Lisa said. "It would be okay with me if you and Dad—"

Panic rose in Adele's throat. Unable to bear hearing the rest, she shook her head. "Oh, no, Lisa. Not—"

"I see you got your gift," Jason said from behind her.

Adele felt another clutch of emotion and whirled around. "Yes. It's wonderful," she said, and felt the threat of tears. She bit her lip and pressed a fingertip just below one of her eyes.

"Can I have another cookie?" Lisa asked, eyeing the dessert table.

"Just one," Jason said sternly, then ruined it by tugging her ponytail as she sped away. He sat next to Adele. "Why are you crying?" he asked in a low voice.

"She made it herself," Adele said, trying unsuccessfully to keep the waver from her voice. "And she gave me a story."

Jason shook his head and chuckled. "Isn't that what you said you wanted?"

"Yes, but—" She shot him a wary glance. "You didn't put her up to this, did you?"

He shook his head again. "No. My daughter can be plenty creative without my input." He studied her face and leaned closer, putting his mouth next to her ear. "Let's leave."

"We haven't been here long."

"I have other plans for you tonight."

His voice made promises she knew he would deliver on. "What kind of plans?"

"I'd rather show you."

Jason couldn't keep his hands off her. As soon as they made it inside his front foyer, he kissed her. He wanted inside her. What was it about this woman that made him want to possess her again and again? What was it about this woman that made him want to give her everything? Was it because he had finally found a woman he could trust?

Reining in the desire that drove him like wildfire, he pulled back and took a deep breath. "You present an ongoing challenge to me."

She licked her lips, and he felt himself grow hard with arousal. "What challenge?"

"I want you," he said, "entirely too much."

"I have the same problem," she said, her gaze locked with his.

Jason bit back an oath at the response she evoked from him and carried her to the master bedroom. He'd promised himself he would go slowly. "The housekeeper's gone, and Lisa's spending the night with my mother. Stay with me."

She gave a breathless laugh.

"What?"

Her green eyes shone with a mix of amusement and desire. "Do you ever ask?"

He gave a put-upon sigh. "Okay, do you want champagne before or after I take off your dress?"

"Are you saying you don't like my dress?" she asked as he allowed her to slide down onto her tiptoes.

Jason shook his head. The burgundy velvet hugged her curves tantalizingly and made her hair look like fire. "It's a beautiful dress. It's just in my way."

"Do you always have to be in control?" she asked, playing with his bolo string tie.

"If I always had to be in control," he said wryly, "I sure as hell wouldn't choose to be with you."

"Then let me take a turn," she said.

"A turn doing what?"

"Being in control," she said, and pulled the silver-and-turquoise slide all the way down to the knotted tips of his bolo.

She wore a look of challenge in her eyes that made him feel like growling, but he swallowed the urge. "Let's take turns," he agreed, knowing he was operating on a short leash.

"Okay," she said with a siren's smile. "Me first."

Eleven

The expression in her eyes made him hard. Tempted to make Adele's "turn" very brief, Jason took a quick, short breath. "Champagne first," he said, counting on the cool, sparkling wine to take the edge off his gnawing need for her. He quickly grabbed the chilled champagne and glasses from the kitchen and returned to her.

Popping the cork, he reached for the glasses, but she only held out one.

Her siren smile returned. "Let's share."

Jason poured the champagne. Watching Adele as she took a few swallows and licked her lips, he felt a little more of the control he so valued slip from his fingertips.

She lifted the glass to his lips. He covered her

hand with his and finished the rest of the cool, bub-
bly liquid. He poured one more glass, and when she
shook her head, he downed it.

Adele took the bottle and glass from his hand and
set them on the coffee table. "I always heard you
weren't supposed to drink champagne quickly. I
thought you were supposed to sip it slowly," she
said as she took her time unbuttoning his shirt.

"I could use a couple of shots of whisky," he
admitted, weaving his fingers through her hair and
pretending not to notice as her hand hovered at his
belt buckle. "If I had my way, I'd take you on the
floor right now."

Her gaze met his, and he felt the strength of his
hunger for her mirrored back at him through her
eyes. Spreading her hands over his chest, she lifted
her mouth to his. "Why do I want you so much?"
she whispered, the question a mixture of tortured
desire and something deeper.

Her lips touched a chord deep inside him, making
his chest contract. Jason had always known Adele's
appeal to him went deeper than her body, but there
had been a time when he'd told himself that pos-
sessing her physically would assuage his need. She
seduced his mouth, kissing him as if she couldn't
get enough of him. Him. As if she couldn't get
enough of Jason Fortune, the man. The knowledge
was irresistible to him.

Jason returned her caresses, consuming her lips
and tongue, taking her mouth the way he wanted to
take her body. He lowered one of his hands to her
breast and found the nipple stiff beneath the velvet.

Adele's moan stirred something elemental in him. She pulled back slightly. ''You make me forget it's my turn,'' she said with a trembling smile.

Jason withheld a groan as she skimmed her hands down to the top of his slacks and unbuckled his belt, unbuttoned, and slowly slid the zipper down.

She brushed her lips against his again as she cupped him and caressed him. She rubbed her thumb over the tip of him and Jason began to sweat. Her small, but, oh, so capable hand rubbed him until his mind clouded with nothing but Adele. He wanted her body, he wanted her mind, he wanted her soul. With a strength that frustrated and threatened him, he wanted her. He wanted everything about her: her impudence, her sense of humor, her beauty and sensuality. Was it possible, he wondered, to absorb all of her being into his at once? Would he at last feel complete?

The question shot out of nowhere, undoing him further. He had always believed he was complete, that he didn't need a woman. God help him, what if he was wrong?

Torn by his overwhelming arousal and the disturbing depth of his desire for Adele, he took her mouth and kissed her with urgency.

Adele shook her head, and frustration stung him. ''How long does your turn last?'' he asked, hearing the growl in his voice.

''I'm not done yet,'' she said and skimmed her mouth down his chest, darting her tongue, singeing his nerve endings with each touch. Rubbing her hair against his bare skin, she lowered her mouth to his belly, and Jason felt his gut clench in anticipation. He had visualized this too many nights to count.

Barely sucking in a quick breath, he watched her as she pressed her open mouth against his arousal. She dragged her tongue from the base of him all the way to the top, then took him fully into her mouth. The sight of her lips on him was so erotic he almost couldn't watch. She pumped gently and he began to swear, a combination of oath and prayer. Pushed to the edge, unable to bear the sight and sensation one more moment, he withdrew and pulled her up to him, taking her mouth. She tasted of his essence, and the knowledge drove him wild.

"You didn't like it?" she asked uncertainly.

Jason groaned. "Too much," he said, and lowered her zipper, dress and panties in one fell swoop. "My turn now."

He luxuriated in the silky skin of her breasts, back and bottom. Squeezing her hips, he rubbed her against the part of him she'd made ache while he made love to her mouth. He felt her knees dip against his and her vulnerability caught at his heart. "Wrap your legs around me," he told her, and carried her to his bedroom.

Her wet femininity hovered just above him, tempting him. More than anything he wanted to ease her down and plunge into her velvet wetness. On the fringes of his mind, however, he knew he had to protect her. He had to protect himself. Deeper still, he wanted nothing between them.

Easing her onto his bed, he watched her hair fan out on either side as her eyes glowed with a wild fire. She rubbed her thighs together and bit her lip as if she were trying to keep from saying something.

Jason grabbed a couple of plastic packets from the bedside table and quickly applied one for protection. "What is it?" he asked her as she lifted her trembling hand to his face.

She closed her eyes and shook her head.

"Look at me," he demanded, craving the ultimate connection with her. "What is it?"

She opened eyes full of fear and forever, and he plunged inside her. She shuddered. "I'm not supposed to love you," she confessed in a broken voice that wrenched at him. "But I do. I love you."

Her words rocked him. He wanted to give her everything she'd never had. He wanted to be every person she'd ever needed. On either side of her, he deliberately twined his fingers through hers and began a rhythm that took him higher and higher. He felt himself getting lost in her eyes as her body intimately massaged him.

Nearing the crest, he hung suspended, as if one of his feet were on a cliff and the other off. She cried out his name, and the sound drew a primitive satisfaction from his gut, his heart, his loins. The pleasure whipped through him like a flame, like the flame in his dream. Just before he flew, it hit him that for all his taking, he had been taken, too.

The next morning Jason awakened to the sensation of Adele's curls brushing his shoulder and her hand resting over his heart. The knowledge that she was naked made him want to make love to her again. Glancing at his alarm clock, he sighed. He hadn't been to the office in several days due to his trip to L.A., and he knew there were several minor crises waiting for his attention.

He wondered when he would get enough of her. He wondered *if* he would get enough of her. She generated an odd combination of emotions inside him, contentment, desire, challenge and protectiveness. He didn't want her to return to Minnesota. He would find a way to make her job permanent. The decision eased something inside him, and he reached over to gently kiss her forehead.

Her eyelids fluttered, and the way she instinctively curled around him squeezed his heart. Again he wanted to make love to her. "You're so beautiful you could make it very difficult for a man to get to work in the morning."

She looked at him in disbelief. "Beautiful? In the morning? I don't even want to think what my hair looks like. How long have you needed glasses?"

Jason chuckled. "My vision is better than perfect. It's 20/15 in both eyes."

She buried her head in his shoulder. "Better than perfect. Why doesn't that surprise me? The rest of us lesser mortals content ourselves with mere 20/20 vision, but not you, Your Highness."

"If I were truly a desert prince, you would have been in big trouble for your impertinence many times since you've arrived in Pueblo. I like the idea of being able to tell you what to do on occasion."

She glanced up at him with a dark look in her eyes. "I guess everyone needs a fantasy."

Jason chuckled again and slid his hand down her silky body to gently squeeze her bottom. "We need to get up," he said regretfully. "I need to go to work early this morning."

"Not me. I have an appointment."

He sat up. "With who?"

"Doctor."

Jason frowned and studied her. "Is something wrong?"

Her face bloomed with color. "I'm going on the Pill."

A little rush of pleasure surged through him. He nodded in approval and reached down to kiss her. "Good. Stop by and see me after you arrive in the office."

"Won't you be too busy?"

He didn't say that seeing her would make his day ten times better, but he thought it. "No. I'll be looking for you."

"Miss O'Neil, I must tell you that according to the test we ran upon your arrival this morning, you won't be needing birth control pills."

Gripping the leather upholstery of the chair in the doctor's private office, Adele stared in confusion at the compassion on the woman's face. She'd completed the exam and was ready to be on her way. "Pardon?"

Dr. Carolyn Wingfield set down Adele's chart and folded her hands. "Due to the dates of your last menstrual cycle and the fact that you're late, we gave you a pregnancy test and it was positive."

The room began to spin. "Positive?"

Dr. Wingfield nodded. "Yes, you're pregnant."

"But I can't—" She swallowed over a suddenly dry throat. "I—" They had always used protection, hadn't they? There hadn't ever been a time in the dark middle of the night when they'd forgotten, had there? Adele searched her memory, but everything seemed fuzzy. "I don't know how…" she began, and closed her mouth. Of course, she knew *how* babies were made.

Dr. Wingfield's forehead creased in sympathy. "This is obviously a shock. You don't have to do anything. It's very early in the pregnancy. You don't have to make any decisions just yet."

"Decisions!" Adele echoed, panic slicing through her.

"I suggest you take the rest of the day and catch your breath. From a medical standpoint, the only thing I want you to start immediately is your pre-natal vitamins, and we have some samples that will last a week." She filled out a prescription and handed it to Adele. "Make an appointment for next month. If you need to see me sooner, don't hesitate to call. You're in superb health. We can make re-ferrals to counselors if you need additional help. But today you just need to breathe."

Adele was still trying to breathe by the time she walked into her condo. *Pregnant.* Her breath caught in her throat for the hundredth time. Pacing through the kitchen and den, she racked her brain for when it could have happened. Did it really matter when?

she asked herself. When it happened didn't change the fact that it had.

She was pregnant.

Adele covered her face with her hands. She had never visualized this for herself, at least not since she'd been a very young girl. Long ago she had decided she hadn't received the training necessary to be a mother, and she refused to inflict her ignorance on an innocent child. Now she was left with no choice.

Lord, she wished she had someone to talk to. But there was no one. Adele tried to think of one person with whom she could share this. Jasmine Fortune's expressive, compassionate face floated into Adele's mind, but she shook her head. In another time, Adele thought. In another situation, but not this one.

The clock struck ten o'clock, and the panic closed in around her again. Jason was expecting her. Adele bit her lip. She couldn't face him. She couldn't imagine telling him. She couldn't imagine not telling him. Her knees began to tremble, and she sank onto the sofa. She reached for the phone and punched out his number. A sliver of relief eased through her when his assistant answered.

"This is Adele O'Neil," Adele said.

"Oh, Adele, I'll put you right through. Jason said to send you in as soon as you arrive."

"Don't do that!" Adele said, and winced at the desperate tone in her voice. She took a small breath. "I'm sure Jason is very busy today. Just please let him know that I'll be in tomorrow, but I won't be in today. Thanks so much. 'Bye now," she said, and hung up determined to collect her thoughts during the time she'd just bought herself.

After an excruciatingly long, busy day, Jason called Adele for the third time at 6 p.m. and frowned at the sound of continued ringing. He waited a few extra rings, then hung up the phone. He had an unsettling gnawing sensation in his gut that had nothing to do with his need for dinner.

He couldn't explain it, but he had a feeling about Adele. It was strong, almost supernatural, and it bothered the hell out of him. Although he'd successfully plowed through his work, she had hovered on the fringes of his mind. He'd expected her to walk through his office door throughout the afternoon even after his assistant had told him Adele wouldn't be in today.

A knock sounded on his door, and Tyler breezed in. "Want to go for a beer and steak? I can give you an update on the construction progress and the investigation. I think we're in good hands with Link Templeton. That's one sharp investigator."

Jason snapped the top on his Mont Blanc pen and stood. "Rain check on dinner, and I'll take the update in the morning."

Tyler nodded with a speculative look on his face. "Dinner with the redhead?"

"Nothing planned, just following my gut," he said, shrugging into his suit coat.

Tyler rubbed his chin. "You look worried. Is something wrong?"

"I don't know," Jason said. "I just have a weird feeling about her."

"Adele?"

"Yeah."

"You sound like Dad. He gets those *feelings* sometimes."

"It's probably nothing," Jason said, even though he didn't believe it. He was impatient to see Adele.

"Yeah, well let me know if it's monumental," Tyler said with a skeptical expression on his face as he backed out of the office. "Later."

Jason nodded, but his mind was already five miles down the road at Adele's condo.

Adele pulled into a parking place in front of her condo and took a deep breath. It had taken a drive to Tucson and back, a light dinner and her first pre-natal vitamin, but she was finally breathing almost normally. She glanced up at the moon and stars in the Arizona sky and thought again about the crazy turn her life had taken. She knew she was facing the biggest challenge of her life. Wrapping her arms around herself, she thought it would be nice if, this once, she didn't have to face it alone.

Getting out of the car, she walked toward her condo.

"I missed you. Why did you play hooky?" Jason asked from behind her.

Adele's heart bolted. She stopped and bit her lip. "I needed a little extra time today, and I thought you'd be too busy playing catch-up to accomplish much on the hospital policies."

He stood beside her, and she felt his gaze but couldn't bring herself to meet it. "But I wanted to see you."

She shrugged.

She saw him shove his fists into his pockets. "So where did you go? How was your doctor appointment?"

Adele's chest tightened. She hadn't decided how to tell Jason. She was just getting used to the idea that she was pregnant herself. "I had my appointment, then this afternoon I drove to Tucson, ate a light dinner and drove back."

Silence stretched uncomfortably between them. "Adele, there's something going on, something you're not telling me. I want to know what it is." He paused. "Are you seeing someone else?"

Surprise shot through her. She met his gaze. "Oh, for Heaven's sake, no!"

His face was full of resolve. "Then what?"

Adele sighed. "I'm a little tired. I think I could handle this better another time."

"This what?"

Loathe to tell him, she shook her head. "Not now."

"Then when?"

"I don't know. I haven't figured that out. I'm still adjusting to—"

"Dammit, Adele. Tell me what is going on. If it's not another man, what is it?"

He paused a half beat, and Adele would have sworn his gaze held the power of lasers, seeing straight through her. "You didn't say how your doctor appointment was this morning."

Adele crossed her arms over her chest. "The doctor said I was in perfect health."

"So you got the pills," he concluded.

"No," she reluctantly admitted.

"Why?" he demanded.

Adele was struck by the knowledge that she would never want to be on the opposite side of a fight with this man. He was relentless. "Come inside," she finally said, and led the way into her condo. She felt frozen with fear and her own disbelief, but Adele knew she was going to have to tell Jason. She might as well get it over with.

As soon as he closed the door behind him, she turned toward him. "The reason I didn't get the birth control pills is because I'm pregnant."

Shock widened his eyes. "You can't be." He hesitated a sliver of a moment, and his gaze hardened. "Unless there's another man."

Adele gasped. "Absolutely not. There's been no one but you. How could you think that? I've been consumed with you. I—" She swallowed over her indignation. "You have been the only man to make love to me in over a year."

"You can't be pregnant," he insisted. "We used protection every time. I made damn sure of it."

"That's what I thought," Adele said. "I've spent the afternoon racking my brain, remembering every time we—" Her voice faltered and she looked away. "That first night, in the middle of the night, I wondered if I had dreamed it. Now I don't think I was dreaming. We weren't all the way awake. It was all instinct and need. I don't remember using protection."

Silence hung thickly between him. Jason swore and turned away. His reaction hurt, even though Adele knew she had felt the same way. "What are you going to do?"

"What do you mean?"

"Are you going to keep the baby?"

Adele instinctively covered her abdomen. She had thought about her choices. After all, she had been the result of an unwed affair, and her childhood had been less than ideal. She had been committed to not having children of her own, but now that she was pregnant, she could not imagine not doing everything in her power to protect and love this baby.

"Yes, I'm going to keep the baby. I don't have everything figured out, but you don't need to worry that I'll ask anything of you. I can handle this on my own," she said in a voice that sounded much stronger than she felt.

Jason didn't pause. "We'll get married immediately."

Adele's heart stuttered. In her heart of hearts, she had wanted to belong to Jason, but not this way. "It's not necessary. There are much, much worse things than having a well-educated single mother who tries her best."

He narrowed his eyes and shook his head. "In various ways I've watched my family suffer from the results of illegitimacy. No child of mine will ever have to bear that burden."

Adele didn't hear an ounce of give in his voice. "I'm not sure raising a child with parents who felt forced to marry each other is the best option."

"You're already pregnant, so the best option," Jason said bluntly, "is not available. Getting married as quickly as possible will provide the best protection for the child. What if something happened to you? You have to think beyond today, Adele. A child needs two parents. You wouldn't want your child to end up in a children's home the way you did, would you?"

The very thought of it sickened her. "No," she said, shaking her head. "No, not that."

"Then we'll be married," Jason said, his voice ringing with finality.

Adele looked at his hard face and felt as if someone had closed her inside a steel vault. He was clear-headed, as if this were a contract negotiation. A business deal. Her stomach turned again. Their marriage would be a business deal.

Twelve

Three days later Adele struggled with a foot problem. Her toes never seemed to get warm. Cold feet. Every time she thought of marrying Jason, her feet grew colder.

He hadn't touched her since she'd told him about the pregnancy. She wondered if he blamed her. She certainly blamed herself. She should have been more careful. Now his life was turned upside down, and so was hers. Funny, though, she wasn't nearly as concerned about the havoc having a child would wreak in her life as she was concerned about the idea of the business marriage. In fact, with each new day, Adele was filled with the peace that she would do whatever it took to love and protect this baby. There was nothing she wouldn't do for the baby;

although, sometimes at night she wondered if marrying Jason in these circumstances was the best choice.

Today was diamond day, she thought as Jason drove her to the finest jeweler in Pueblo. Courteous as ever, he held the door for her and escorted her inside the exclusive shop. "You should choose something you like," he told her. "You'll be wearing it a long time."

Adele tensed. His words sounded more like a sentence.

The jeweler led Adele and Jason to the back of his shop. "Congratulations to both of you," he said, and pulled out a tray of diamond rings. "These are our finest."

Adele felt a chill as she looked at the stones. They looked so cold. She shook off the thought and lifted her lips in a small smile. "They're beautiful."

The jeweler pulled out a platinum ring with a large emerald-cut stone and baguettes. "What do you think of this?" he asked, and slid the elaborate ring on her finger.

"It's too big," she murmured.

"It can be sized," Jason said.

"No, that's not—" She tried for a smile again, but it was harder this time. She returned the ring to the jeweler. "It's beautiful, but I don't think it's me."

"What about this one?" the jeweler asked, eager to please. He pulled out a brilliant diamond, set in yellow gold encrusted with pearls and diamonds.

The setting was elaborate, almost to the point of being gaudy.

Adele shook her head. "I don't think so."

And so it went for the next twenty-five minutes. Adele could feel the growing exasperation shared by both the jeweler and Jason, and the tension inside her pulled tighter with each passing moment. "I think we need to try this another time," she finally announced. "Perhaps you have a brochure and I could look at the pictures. That way I might get a better idea of what I truly like."

The jeweler sagged with relief. "I'll get one for you to take with you."

Within moments Jason thanked the jeweler for his time, and he and Adele left the store. As he joined her in the car, he looked at her as if his patience was stretched. "You didn't like any of them?" he asked in disbelief. "The first one was four carats."

"The man had some beautiful stuff, Jason," she said, lifting her chin. "But it's still just stuff," she told him, thinking of the story she'd told him about her childhood.

"You need an engagement ring," he said.

She laughed. "No, I don't *need* a ring. I need shelter, clothing, food, self-respect, a sense of purpose and a few good friends." And I would like to be loved, a tiny voice in the back of her mind whispered, but Adele snuffed it out. She refused to dwell on a wish that was clearly going to remain unfulfilled.

"We can get your ring another day," he said in a voice that mixed stretched patience and steely resolve. "But I think we should be married within a week, so we need to go ahead and make plans for the wedding."

Adele's blood ran cold. "One week," she said in dismay. "There's no rush."

"Yes, there is," he insisted, starting the ignition and driving out of the parking lot. "You're not getting less pregnant."

"But it's not as if I'll be showing anytime soon, either."

"People count weeks and months and compare them with anniversary dates. The sooner we marry, the easier it will be for the baby. I'd planned to spring the news on my parents tonight after we got your ring. I'm sure my mother will be delighted to help put together a small ceremony. Where would you like it held?"

Numb, Adele shook her head. "I hadn't thought about it. Why don't we just do something with a justice of the peace?"

"We could," Jason said. "But I think it might be better in the long run if my parents and Lisa were included in the celebration."

If this was supposed to be a celebration, why did it feel like a funeral? Adele's qualms increased. "Are you sure we can't wait a little longer?"

"I'm sure," he said. "I've done this before."

Adele blinked. "What do you mean?"

"You may have forgotten, but the first time I got married, the situation was similar. Cara was pregnant, too."

Adele was cut to the quick that she would be a

constant reminder to Jason of the pain of his first marriage. She could see that she had gone from being a joy to a burden, and she wasn't sure she could bear it.

That night, after dinner, he took her to his parents' expansive ranch on the outskirts of Pueblo. The polished wood and Southwestern decor gave the impression of luxurious warmth and tradition.

"You didn't eat much at dinner," Jason said in a hushed voice as they entered his parents' foyer.

Dinner had been uncomfortably quiet. "I guess I was a little edgy."

"My parents like you," he said. "They'll be pleased."

Adele bit her tongue for a second, then her forthright nature took over. "I'm not sure they're the problem."

He did a double take. "Lisa was ecstatic when we told her earlier."

"Yes, but what about Jason?" Adele asked.

A muscle in his cheek twitched. "I'm doing the right thing."

Honor above all, Adele thought, and her heart just plain hurt. She stifled a sigh as Jason's father approached them. Jason slipped his arm around her shoulders. "I have some news," he said. "Where's Mom?"

"Right here," Jasmine said, rounding the corner, her eyes bright with curiosity. She hooked her arm through her husband's. "Come into the den."

Her stomach a jumble of nerves, Adele walked

with Jason into the den. His parents sat, but he didn't. "Adele and I have decided to get married," he announced.

Jasmine clasped her hands together in delight. Her eyes shone. "Oh, Jason, how wonderful!" She quickly stood and hugged both Jason and Adele. "I'm so happy. I know you two will be so happy together."

"Thank you," Adele murmured, and swallowed over a knot in her throat. Jasmine was so sincerely happy for them that she felt guilty. If Jason's mother knew everything, she might not be nearly so pleased.

"Champagne," Jasmine said. "Devlin, I think this calls for a toast."

"I'll get the bottle we keep chilled in the refrigerator," Devlin said, and briefly left the room.

"This is so exciting," Jasmine said. "Have you set a date?"

"We'd like to do something small," Jason said. "Soon."

"How soon?" Devlin asked as he returned with the champagne and glasses.

"One week or less."

Jasmine gasped. "One week! There's so much to do."

Devlin smiled indulgently. "If you need any help with arrangements, you might be able to twist her arm." He turned his attention to Adele and studied her.

Adele had the same uncomfortable sensation she'd felt when Jason had looked at her the same way just a few days ago. It was as if Devlin could see straight through her. A strong compassion, however, emanated from him.

"Welcome," he said simply, and hugged her.

Adele was so moved by the loving openness of Jason's family that she felt tears threaten. Over Devlin's shoulder she met Jason's distant gaze and wondered again if they were doing the right thing.

After fifteen minutes of toasting and a silent drive home, Jason escorted her to her door. "I think it went well," he said. "Why didn't you drink the champagne?"

Surprised he'd noticed, Adele tossed him a sideways glance. She'd had to pretend to drink. It seemed pretending was becoming the norm. "I'm pregnant. I have to cut out alcohol."

He stared at her. "Cara didn't."

"I'm not Cara," she said.

"No, you're not," he agreed, but he still didn't touch her, and his eyes held shadows of pain.

The wedding dress hanging on the front of the coat closet door mocked her. Jasmine had been only too delighted to help Adele select the dress. She had also been delighted to help make the other wedding arrangements, too. Jasmine had been far more delighted than Adele had been, and Adele was done with pretending. Jasmine's genuine affection made Adele feel shallow and just plain icky.

Fifteen minutes ago as she'd stared at that wedding dress, Adele had reached an important decision. Before she could lose her nerve, she'd called Jason and asked him to come over as soon as he could comfortably fit it in his schedule.

Adele glanced at the clock again and felt an attack of nerves. "You have to do this," she told herself. "It may not seem like it's the best thing, but it is."

The doorbell rang, and she nearly jumped out of her skin. Taking a careful breath, she walked to the door and opened it to Jason. Her heart jolted at the sight of him. Would it always do that? she wondered. "Thank you for coming so quickly."

Walking into the condo, he studied her. "It sounded urgent."

Feeling her nerves rattle again, she clasped her hands together. "Not really urgent, just necessary."

He glanced around the room, and his gaze stopped at the sight of her wedding dress. He deliberately glanced away. "I see you've been shopping with my mother. I think I'm not supposed to see that before the wedding day. Bad luck or something."

Adele waved her hand dismissingly. "It doesn't matter. I'm not wearing it, anyway."

"Pardon?" he asked in a deep voice that reminded her how seductive he could be.

"Sit down," she said, waving her hand again.

"Excuse me?"

"Please," Adele said. "Please just sit down and listen."

Jason did, and Adele felt his gaze on her in a wary, yet predatory manner. She had his attention, she thought. Now what was she supposed to do?

Rolling her eyes at herself, she began to pace. "I've been thinking. A lot," she added. "A long time ago there was nothing I wanted more than to have my own family. I wanted to grow up and have a husband and children, people who needed me and wanted me. People who loved me. Back when I was a little girl, I couldn't imagine anything more wonderful than belonging to a family. I used to fantasize about it for hours. As I grew older I put that dream aside. Being around you and your wonderful family, though, brought it all up for me again. As much as I told myself you and I would never marry, I think a little part of me wished I could belong to you and you could belong to me.''

Forced to take a breath, Adele felt heat rush to her face at her confession. She couldn't look at Jason. "For a long time I thought there couldn't be anything worse than not belonging to somebody. But I think I may have been wrong. I think pretending to belong is a lot worse. You're a wonderful man, but you've been miserable as hell since you decided we should get married.''

She heard her voice crack with emotion, and bit her lip. She finally met his gaze. "I can't marry you.''

Jason stood, his expression incredulous. "What on earth are you talking about?''

Her heart hammered in her chest. "I can't marry you. I refuse to make you miserable, and pretending that I belong when I really don't would make me miserable.''

"I'm not miserable because I'm marrying you," Jason said.

"It sure looks that way. Do you realize you have

not touched me since I told you I was pregnant?'' she asked, her voice and hands trembling. She prayed she wouldn't cry, but that had hurt her so.

He winced as if in pain. ''Cara didn't want me to touch her after she got pregnant.''

Adele saw the remnants of damage from his first marriage in his bleak gaze. ''I thought we'd already covered that I'm not Cara,'' she said gently.

''But I got you pregnant and we weren't married,'' Jason said.

''And I believe that is where any similarities end,'' Adele said.

''She didn't want to have Lisa,'' he told her. ''I pushed her. She probably died because of it.''

Adele's head reeled. ''She didn't want to have your baby?''

''Cara had diabetes, and she wasn't always conscientious with her treatment. She had a miscarriage soon after we married. When she got pregnant with Lisa, I hoped it might bring us closer. No matter how much I hounded her, she didn't take care of herself during her pregnancy. It caused a lot of damage.''

''You blame yourself,'' Adele said.

''Some,'' he admitted, and the hollow expression in his eyes scraped her soul. ''I couldn't bear it if it happened to you.''

Her heart could have wept. She walked closer to him. ''It's not going to happen to me. I don't have diabetes. I'm going to take care of myself and this baby. Haven't you ever heard the expression 'The good die young, but mean is forever'? I'm mean,'' she said cheerfully. "The last time I got a cold was eight years ago. I'm so disgustingly healthy it makes a lot of people sick. In fact, the doctor said that if my pregnancy progresses as expected, she thinks I could use a midwife at home."

His face paled. "Absolutely not. You'll have our baby in the hospital where you'll be safe."

"The natural way God intended," Adele said in a wry voice.

"You will marry me," Jason said, stepping toward her.

Adele sighed. "There you go with the orders again," she murmured. "You can't make me. I love you too much to make you miserable by marrying me."

Jason raked his hand through his hair. "You're the most exasperating woman I've ever met. I'm not miserable. I'll be miserable if you don't marry me."

Adele crossed her arms over her chest, but leaned into his personal space. "I love you," she said, "but I don't believe you."

Jason looked into her eyes and felt the familiar drag of dare and challenge. He pulled her against him and took her mouth. "I can't lose you, Adele. I feel as if I've found a part of myself I never knew existed in you. I can't lose you."

After drowning in dread and isolation all week, to Jason, Adele's arms felt like Heaven.

"Why did you stop holding me?" Adele asked, holding tight, yet pulling slightly away so she could look into his face. "I thought you didn't want me anymore."

Jason's heart broke in two. He covered her lips with his finger. "No, not that. All I could think about was what had happened last time and that I had royally messed up again."

"But it's the best kind of mess up, Jason. As much as you and I absolutely didn't plan this, I believe this baby is a gift."

Her words and touch filled him with a peace he'd never known. "I love you," he said. "I never knew how alone I didn't have to feel."

He watched tears spill from her eyes and tried to catch them with his fingers. He could see the magic his words caused in her, and he wished he hadn't held them back so long. He wished he hadn't been so doubtful. When he looked at Adele, Jason knew with a deep sense of eternity that he could trust her, that he could trust what they had together. "I love you," he repeated. "Please marry me."

She swiped at her cheeks. "I thought I bothered you."

"You do," he said. "And I want you to bother me for the rest of my life."

After that momentous night Jason hadn't stopped touching her and reminding her that he loved her, and Adele had never been happier. Every once in a while she saw the worry flicker in his eyes, but she kissed it away. Their marriage ceremony was scheduled for the following morning, and the family had attended an informal rehearsal dinner just hours before. Jason, however, had insisted on a secret outing, instructing Adele to dress warmly for the cool night.

He drove the borrowed Jeep past the construction site, then down a dirt road and stopped. He looked at her with a mysterious glint in his eyes. "Ready?" he asked.

Her heart thumped at the seductive expression. Adele suspected it always would. "What are we doing?" she asked as he led her out of the car and helped her over a dilapidated wooden fence.

"Trespassing," he said.

Adele stumbled. "Okeydoke," she said, still literally and figuratively in the dark. "I realize most people have a bachelor party the night before their wedding, but I'm obviously not familiar with all the possible traditions."

"It's a family tradition," he told her, surprising her.

"Tell me about it," she said, slipping her hand in his as they walked across the desert. A full moon shone on the barren landscape.

Jason pointed his flashlight up ahead. "There it is," he said, squeezing her hand.

"What—" Adele broke off when she remembered the familiar site. "The picture on your wall," she said. "Lightfoot's Plateau."

A simple structure of adobe bricks stood in front of the cave. "The Lightfoot family have been the guardians of the plateau for centuries. Natasha's mother and father were the last couple to pledge themselves within the cave. When my grandmother Natasha gave birth out of wedlock, her family was disgraced within the community. They refused to let

Natasha inherit the land and instead sold it. We intend to get it back.''

''I can feel that it's a special place.''

Jason led her toward the opening of the cave. ''The legend about this plateau is that if a man and woman would come to the cave to pledge themselves to each other, through their pledge, their love would then become pure and last a lifetime.''

Adele looked into the fiercely protective, loving eyes of the man she would cherish forever. ''That's why you brought me here.''

''I love you, Adele. I believe that I was made for you and you for me. I will do my best to help make you happier than you've ever dreamed. I will always belong to you.''

His words healed the deepest wounds in her soul. ''I am so in awe of you,'' she said. ''I want to spend my life making sure you never forget what an incredible man you are. I will always love you. I will always be here for you.''

Jason pulled something shiny from his pocket. ''I had this ring made for you, since you were so picky about the other ones,'' he said in a voice more tender than dry. He pointed his flashlight on the platinum ring that featured a sparkling diamond set off by diamond baguettes and turquoise. ''The turquoise belonged to Natasha Lightfoot, my grandmother.''

Adele's heart overflowed with emotion. Her eyes welled with tears. ''Not just stuff. It's incredible. You did it again,'' she whispered. ''You gave me a story.''

He pulled her against him and made one more

vow. "I've just started, Adele. I'll be giving you stories the rest of your life."

The following morning dawned bright and clear. Jason stood at the front of the archway and watched his daughter bounce down the aisle in excitement. Adele appeared, a vision in a simple white gown. Her red hair was a flame of curls, and her green eyes were only for him.

She walked toward him, and Jason felt no last-minute trepidation, only eagerness to begin their life together. He still had trouble believing he had found his soul mate, the woman who matched him in fire and strength. He wanted her by his side day and night. He craved the completion she gave him.

She smiled, and he wanted her with a power that he suspected would always shake him. As if she knew exactly what he was feeling, she stepped forward and kissed him, reassuring and claiming him with the brief caress. He heard a few chuckles sweep over the small crowd of family at her boldness, but he could only smile.

"Am I bothering you?" she whispered.

"Oh, yes," he murmured. "In the very best way."

As he and Adele made their public vows, he remembered the private vows they'd made the night before, and Jason knew he had found a love to last a lifetime. He also knew that the real love and real work to make that love grow was just beginning.

* * * * *

Want to find out what happens to Tyler?
Look for Julie and Tyler Fortune's
love story in

MAIL-ORDER CINDERELLA

by Kathryn Jensen
Coming to Silhouette Desire's
Fortune's Children: The Grooms
miniseries in September.

And now for a sneak preview of
MAIL-ORDER CINDERELLA,
please turn the page.

One

Tyler Fortune hated losing a fight, and today he'd lost big-time. Now he was going to pay for it, and the price was...marriage.

His sole consolation was that he would relinquish freedom on his own terms. He'd be damned if he let his parents corral him into marrying a snooty Tucson debutante or one of their wealthy friends' daughters.

Tensing at the thought of the complications a wife and family would inflict on his well-ordered bachelor life, Tyler viciously jammed his thumb down on the eject button. Out popped the fifth videotape.

"Last one of the batch. You'd better be a winner, sweetheart," Tyler muttered as he slid in the final cartridge and hit Play.

"Doesn't seem to have much of a plot," a low voice stated from the open doorway.

Tyler looked around with a laconic smile at his brother Jason. "Not s'posed to," he drawled, turning back to find a pale, oval face on the TV screen. He stared, surprised by what he saw. This one was…different.

The young woman spoke quietly, almost as if afraid someone might hear her. She wasn't trying to sell herself or flirt with the camera as the other women before her had. She appeared not to have worn any makeup at all, but the harsh studio lights might have washed out a light application. No jewelry of any kind was evident at her throat, earlobes or wrists. If one word described her, it was *plain*.

Nevertheless, something about the woman pulled at Tyler, held his gaze, captured his attention just as strongly as the others hadn't.

Jason scowled. "Is this a new technique for interviewing receptionists?"

"Brides."

His brother's sudden laughter rocked the room. "Yeah, right." Jason gasped to catch his breath and wiped at his eyes. "Brides."

"I'm serious. If I have to marry in less than a year, I'll be damned if I'm going to let anyone pick out a wife for me. I tried to tell Dad I'm not cut out for marriage, but he won't listen. And I just don't have time to do this any other way."

"Look at her, you'd think the interviewer was a lion about to devour her."

"She does look about to jump out of her skin,"

Tyler admitted. Her eyes were huge and blinked, blinked, blinked…like those of a wild animal startled by headlights. She repeatedly moistened her lips with the tip of her tongue. For once the gesture didn't look contrived or seductive. Nevertheless, Tyler found it appealing, innocently tantalizing. He'd have settled for seeing her jump out of her clothes.

Now he couldn't take his eyes from the timid woman's face. "Julie," he heard the off-screen interviewer ask her, "why did you apply to Soulmate Search?"

She straightened her spine, hitched back her narrow shoulders and lifted her chin to look directly into the camera for the first time. Tyler was certain the effort to make the simple postural adjustments was enormous.

"I want a baby," she said crisply.

Tyler slowly shook his head. Someone ought to tell her that honesty wouldn't get her very far in the dating world.

"You mean," the interviewer suggested, trying to steer her toward a more appealing reply, "you'd like to find your soul mate, someone to share your interests, like gourmet cooking and a love of children?"

"No," Julie said slowly, emphasizing each subsequent word as if it contained a message of its own, "all…I…want…is…a…child. Children actually. Three, four…more if my husband wants them. I adore children."

Julie…what was her last name? Tyler glanced at the letter that had accompanied the tapes. Parker.

Yes, Julie Ann Parker was just too earnest for this sophisticated matchmaking service with its nation-wide offices. Tyler felt embarrassed for her.

"Nice girl. Doesn't have a clue, does she?" Jason admitted as he headed out of the room.

"Huh? Oh…no." Tyler was still thinking about Julie Parker's eyes. He couldn't remember their color—hazel, he thought—but they displayed a neb-ulous quality he would very much like to explore in person. And that flick of soft pink tongue every now and then…

Tyler picked up the telephone and punched in the 800 number on the letter.

She needed a husband; he needed a wife. A sim-ple trade-off.

FORTUNE FAMILY TREE: THE ARIZONA BRANCH

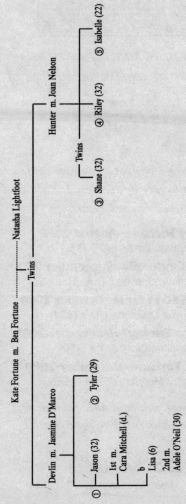

Kate Fortune m. Ben Fortune .... Natasha Lightfoot

Twins

Devlin m. Jasmine D'Marco

① Jason (32) ② Tyler (29)

1st m.
Cara Mitchell (d.)

b

Lisa (6)

2nd m.
Adele O'Neil (30)

Hunter m. Joan Nelson

Twins

③ Shane (32) ④ Riley (32) ⑤ Isabelle (22)

① Bride of Fortune
② Mail-Order Cinderella
③ Fortune's Secret Child
④ Husband —or Enemy?
⑤ Groom of Fortune

d. deceased
..... affair

FORTUNE'S Children™

*The Fortune family requests
your presence at the weddings of*

the Grooms

*Silhouette Desire's provocative new miniseries
featuring the beloved Fortune family and
five of your favorite authors.*

Bride of Fortune—August 2000
by Leanne Banks (SD #1311)

Mail-Order Cinderella—September 2000
by Kathryn Jensen (SD #1318)

Fortune's Secret Child—October 2000
by Shawna Delacorte (SD #1324)

Husband—or Enemy?—November 2000
by Caroline Cross (SD #1330)

Groom of Fortune—December 2000
by Peggy Moreland (SD #1336)

*Don't miss these unforgettable romances . . .
available at your favorite retail outlet.*

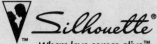

Silhouette®
Where love comes alive™

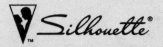

**Don't miss
an exciting opportunity
to save on the purchase of
Harlequin and Silhouette books!**

Buy any two Harlequin or
Silhouette books and save
$10.00 off future Harlequin
and Silhouette purchases

OR

buy any three
Harlequin or Silhouette books
and save **$20.00 off** future
Harlequin and Silhouette purchases.

*Watch for details
coming in October 2000!*

PHQ400

COMING NEXT MONTH

#1315 SLOW WALTZ ACROSS TEXAS—Peggy Moreland
Man of the Month/Texas Grooms
Growing up an orphan had convinced cowboy Clayton Rankin that he
didn't need anyone. But when his wife, Rena, told him he was about to
lose her, he was determined to win back her love—and have his wife
teach him about matters of the heart!

#1316 ROCK SOLID—Jennifer Greene
Body & Soul
She needed to unwind. But when Lexie Woolf saw Cash McKay,
relaxation was the last thing on her mind. Cash was everything Lexie
had dreamed of in a man—except she feared *she* was not the woman
for *him*. Could Cash convince Lexie that their love was rock solid?

#1317 THE NEXT SANTINI BRIDE—Maureen Child
Bachelor Battalion
They were supposed to be together for only one night of passion, but
First Sergeant Dan Mahoney couldn't forget Angela Santini. So he set
out to seduce the single mom—one tantalizing touch at a time—and
convince her that all her nights were meant to be spent with him!

#1318 MAIL-ORDER CINDERELLA—Kathryn Jensen
Fortune's Children: The Grooms
Tyler Fortune needed a bride—and plain librarian Julie Parker fit the
bill. But Tyler never counted on falling for his convenient wife. Now
he needed to convince Julie that she was the perfect mate for him—
so he could become her husband in every way.

#1319 LADY WITH A PAST—Ryanne Corey
She thought no one knew of her former notoriety, but when
Connor Garrett tracked down Maxie Calhoon, she had to face her past.
Connor stirred emotions in Maxie that she had never experienced, but
did he love the woman she once was or the one she had become?

#1320 DOCTOR FOR KEEPS—Kristi Gold
The last thing Dr. Rick Jansen needed was to fall for his new nurse,
Miranda Brooks. Yet there was something about Miranda that made it
impossible to keep his thoughts—and hands—away from her. But
would he still desire Miranda when he learned her secret?

CMN0800